SARTORI

BY

SAM THOMPSON

Copyright© 2020 Sam Thompson Books. All Rights Reserved.

CHAPTER ONE

CHESHIRE –DECEMBER 4th 1997.

The winter sun sat low as it shone over the pretty Cheshire village on the cold December morning. Archbishop Matthew Fitzpatrick was delivering the funeral planned today at St Theresa's church in the quiet village where, Roberto Sartori and his wife lived for the past thirty years.

Archbishop Fitzpatrick did not usually conduct the funerals within the diocese; the parish priests usually had a stronger connection with the congregation at such a personal point in people's lives. This was the first burial service the archbishop had delivered in over twenty years.

Today was different it was for a friend, Roberto Sartori, a devout catholic, along with his wife Antonia and devoted brother, and lifetime business partner Giovanni.

Toni was the driving force in upholding the faith throughout the family; she would often offer large gifts, above twenty thousand pounds, to the diocese. The archbishop was always willing to accept and share a large percentage between the parish priests, whilst allowing his lifestyle to luxuriate a little with any surplus funds he felt appropriate. Roberto knew this and would often make the bishop shuffle with embarrassment.

"In my industry, we would call that creaming off the top." Roberto would say with a smile, he understood the age-old saying 'business is business.'

Roberto was the lead part in today's ceremony following his death weeks earlier after a sudden heart attack, a bullet had not killed him, or a planned gang killing as one would have expected following years of ruthless crime.

Roberto led the family business, which ran undetected for over sixty years. He passed on his godfather status to his grandson William, who made a few mistakes allowing a chink of light through a slightly opened door, the police began to probe, probing into things that made Roberto and Giovanni feel uncomfortable.

The cortege drove slowly through the church gates that sat in a beautiful setting of greenery and hills allowing the sheep to feed, keeping their energy levels high as the winter began to set in with the shorter days and long cold nights.

The fifteenth-century church was very basic in its setting, it was surrounded by a four-foot drywall protecting the multiple headstones, most were overgrown with grass, as relatives themselves passed on from the times the graves were fresh over a hundred and fifty years ago.

Sat in the middle of the cemetery was a large oak tree with a singular high built grave resting beneath it. The grave belonged to Archbishop James Carney placed to rest here in eighteen forty-two, next to it was a freshly dug hole awaiting Roberto, he had donated fifty thousand pounds to secure the plot for him and his family, today it was making its debut.

Toni was a very attractive woman, as a young woman she donned jet-black hair, complimenting her Italian olive coloured skin that most women, would have killed for, today at ninety-four, she was still slim, she remained active and had the energy levels of somebody half her age. Today she wore a calf-length, handmade black dress made of cotton with black broderie anglaise patterns around the collar, the sleeves composed of both round and oval holes. She also wore a simple 24-carat gold necklace that sat on top of the dress, over the dress she wore a jet black handmade woolen coat an inch below the dress length finished off with matching handmade Italian leather court shoes and a clutch bag of which the contents held a pure white handkerchief if required.

The Bentley hearse sat outside the gates of the church as the bells tolled from the square tower, they sat no more than thirty feet high, Toni looked up and saw a huge brass bell swinging in the open building with the sun glistening off it as it swayed back and forth.

Attending were only a handful of mourners, as Roberto wished, Toni and her daughter, Francesca, Giovanni, Edward Le Conte, a close family friend and business partner, along with his wife.

Missing was William Jones, Roberto's grandson, and his wife Margaret, they fled the country following Jonty Ball's skill, as a detective, to close down the families activities, nobody knew where Billy and Maggie had fled and nobody knew if they were going to show up at the funeral of Billy's much-loved grandfather.

Unbeknown to the mourners, also in attendance, hoping Billy would attend, was a police surveillance unit perched high out of sight behind light blue plastic sheeting, the sheets were wrapped around scaffolding which made it look like work was being done to a house fifty yards from the church grounds. Inside the canopy sat on wooden planks used as the floor to oversee the proceedings was detective inspector Jonty Ball. On the police camera was Dan Spencer who had a video camera trained on the churchyard. He was filming every move.

Jonty was a tough-looking man, now in his sixties, with cauliflower ears from years of semi-professional boxing; he stood six foot six inches and weighed in at nineteen stone. Age was not a problem for Jonty as he was still fit and strong; having retired once from the force, he re-joined following the murder of his friend and colleague DI Dave Rowlands.

The familiar sound of a helicopter suddenly came into earshot that a few minutes earlier had been in the distance but was now getting much closer, in fact very close, and very noisy.

Dan spun the camera towards the helicopter and zoomed in, the side doors slid back revealing the letters TV. All the other letters covered by the open doors.

"It looks like a TV film crew have joined us." Dan said to Jonty.

"I'm not surprised; the story grew legs near the end in the media." Jonty replied.

Then in one movement, the chopper took a drastic dive and swooped like a hawk with a vole in its sights, another sharp turn and it was twenty feet above the mourners. The familiar sound of rapid machine guns left the open doors of the helicopter, People were screaming, there was panic from the few mourners in attendance. The first hit was the archbishop, the bullets reigned low and accurate, they first swept across his legs making him fall like a tree being felled in a forest, his hands instinctively went to hold his legs, before a second volley hit him almost instantly this time higher.

There was no mistake he hit the ground as only a dead man could, the helicopter travelled another forty yards gained a little height before turning and swooping again, by now the mourners were running for cover in every direction of the compass. The chopper, rotated a full three hundred and sixty degrees four times as if looking for a target, it then found it. Giovanni was running as fast as his ninety-year-old legs would carry him. The chopper headed for him it was fifty yards, forty, thirty, ten, the machine gun opened its known to all symphony of rat-a-tat-tat. Giovanni dived behind the wall surrounding the church through a gateway used as a side entrance. On the other side of the wall was an old barn, unused for thirty years it was thirty yards away. Easy for a forty-year-old Giovanni, not an older Giovanni, he watched the helicopter fly over releasing a hail of bullets penetrating the wall and surrounding trees, he was safe for now but he knew when the helicopter came in from the opposite direction he would be as open as Bambi in a field surrounded by wolves.

   He made his way to the barn as the helicopter climbed and flew away ready for its turn and second swoop. Giovanni was now halfway and he could tell the helicopter was turning by the noise it made in the air.

   'Do not look for the helicopter it will slow you down.' he thought. He kept moving.

   The helicopter made its swoop again dropping onto its prey. The countryside again interrupted by yet more gunfire that saw the animals in the fields sprint away from the noise and the birds vertically exit the trees in unison.

   'Almost there!' Giovanni thought as he reached the door, his hands were over the doorframe just as a warm tranquil feeling came from his legs, idyllic for a second then the pain, confirming he was hit in the back of the legs. He made one final thrust over the threshold and into the building.

Safe for now, he thought, he looked out of the twenty-foot square opening through the barn door, he could see the helicopter lowering to the ground, they were coming at him again, this time on foot and this time nowhere to hide.

As the helicopter touched the ground the rotors of another helicopter came into earshot, in view was a police helicopter, Jonty had radioed for assistance the second he realised the picture forming in front of him. The helicopter immediately took off, now pursued by the police helicopter.

Jonty made his way to the barn to see if he could help Giovanni. He ran through the opening; which a few minutes earlier had been the barn door, he saw a trail of blood that led to an old man dressed in a black expensive suit, now full of dirt and holes in the knees. the lower part of the trousers were seeping blood that had settled, The sound of sirens became vivid as the ambulance drew up to the barn, just as Dan entered with a shaking of the head, indicating that the archbishop was dead in the cemetery under the leafless oak tree where Roberto was yet to be lowered.

Toni then entered.

"Gio how are you? Who would do this at Roberto's funeral!"

Giovanni looked at Antonia "I am Ok Toni, Just in the legs, I will survive."

"He will be Ok," Steve Rowen, the attending medic said, "We need to get him to a hospital though."

"I am DI Jonty Ball," I was passing the area and saw most of what happened." he lied.

"Did you arrange for the police helicopter?" Toni asked Jonty.

"Yes."

"Thank you because if it had arrived five minutes later Gio would be dead."

The barn had not seen this much activity since the last cow strode out from milking twenty years ago. To add to the increasing crowd Father Luke Hesketh entered the building. He was devastated at the scene he found. He was in tears at the thought of his long-term mentor and friend Archbishop Matthew Fitzpatrick, slain on the sacred ground outside. He kept his composure as he turned to Toni

"If you don't mind Mrs. Sartori, I would like to replace the archbishop and continue with the ceremony for Roberto."

Giovanni nodded, "Roberto would have wanted it." he told Toni squeezing her hand.

She nodded and walked outside where she gave her hysteric daughter, Francesca, a hug and said. "Let's do what we came for. We are Sartori's!"

Father Hesketh offered his prayers to God over the grave of Roberto, the attendees now consisted of Antonia, Francesca, Edward Le Conte, his wife, and Jonty. The activity was rife around the sleepy village, police sirens in the background, and helicopter rotors chugging in the blue winter sky, but the funeral went on, Roberto was slowly lowered into the ground.

Roberto Sartori, laid to rest as he had lived his life, in a field of violence and killings.

The following day Jonty sat down with Dan looking through the footage Dan had taken. It showed the hearse slowly draw up to the church gates, it showed Antonia and Giovanni leave the Bentley car following along with Francesca and Edward Le Conte, Just a normal funeral service. The microphone picked up the unmistakable noise of helicopter rotors in the distance, Jonty asked Dan to stop the footage, Dan did as requested. Jonty pulled out his mobile phone and set the stopwatch on it before asking Dan to restart, Dan continued, as the pictures moved again Jonty clicked the stopwatch into action.

They watched the coffin taken from the hearse and watched the pallbearers place it on their shoulders, they carried it to the side of the grave and lowered it as Archbishop Fitzpatrick walked slowly towards the graveside with a bible opened across his two hands. Archbishops usually wear amaranth red, today he chose purple for the occasion.

They watched as the rotor noise got louder, the first bullet hit Fitzpatrick Jonty told Dan to freeze the screen. He instantly pushed the stop button on the stopwatch.

"Forty seconds." he said, "How can anybody calculate timings so perfect at a funeral, they are not regimented to the second, they are approximate times."

"Can you make it larger and run at a slower speed?" Jonty asked.

Dan set up the video increasing the pixels to zoom in on the pictures then slowed it down to fifty percent of the speed. They sat and watched, the rotors came into earshot as it followed the funeral as Dan made the change from the funeral to the helicopter with the camera, Jonty shouted: "STOP!"

Dan stopped and looked at Jonty.

"Can you go back slide by slide?" Jonty asked.

"Well it's not slide by slide but I can go back through frames."

Dan began to go backward freezing each frame until Jonty gave him the OK to go to the next one.

About forty frames in Jonty said, "Look!"

They could both see a man stood watching on a hill overlooking the funeral but hidden from mourners using a tree as cover, he had a mobile phone to his ear he was talking into it, whilst his vision followed the flight of the helicopter.

"Can you zoom in anymore?" Jonty asked Dan.

"I can try," he answered as he eagerly set the zooms in motion.

The pictures were blurred as it closed in on the man, the shape of a face but no clear definition could be seen through the increased image, certainly not enough to identify him.

"That is the man who is directing the helicopter. He is telling them what stage the funeral is at. That's why the timing was perfect." Jonty told Dan. "All we have to do is find him."

Two days later Jonty went to Salford Royal Hospital to visit Giovanni and see if he was well enough to discuss the attack at the funeral.

He found Giovanni sat up in bed with a case under the bedclothes to protect his legs from the sheets, he also had a block under his ankles preventing his calves from touching the mattress, for a man of his age he was doing well, Giovanni, was strong.

Sat beside him was Toni, Roberto's widow, they had known each other since the prohibition in the nineteen twenties, where Roberto and Giovanni imported top grade Scottish whiskey to the Rossi crime family, fuelling the ever thirsty speakeasies in New York City. She moved to England after meeting and falling in love with Roberto. Giovanni had shared the same large house with them. He enjoyed a few relationships with women but was studious and always enjoyed his own company and the freedom to live without feeling tied down. Different from Roberto who enjoyed the companionship of Toni throughout life.

Giovanni smiled at Jonty as Toni thanked him again for his quick thinking. She told him how lucky they were that he had been in the area.

"Would you like a coffee while you chat with Gio?" she asked Jonty.

"That would be lovely thank you. I can think of nothing I would enjoy more than a hospital vended coffee."

"Well, it's the best you will get today." She answered with a smile.

As she left Jonty turned to Giovanni

"You are an old man now Giovanni, I have no interest in perusing you for your past deeds. I know that it ended sourly with Billy and my intention is to find Billy he is the main suspect for the murder of Paul Jennings."

Giovanni smiled "It's a complex life we lead, I have no idea where William is and even if I did I doubt I would pass on information about the grandson Roberto idolised."

Giovanni looked at Jonty for a second.

"You did well finding out about our business, where did the information come from?" he asked.

"You wouldn't believe it if I told you," Jonty replied

"Try me?"

"Perhaps in the future," Jonty said with a smile.

Jonty pulled out an A4 sized envelope and opened it.

"I have a blurred photograph of a man I think was orchestrating the helicopter attack, it's a very blurred picture but it's the best we have. Do you recognise him?"

Giovanni looked at the picture for a full minute, his face was showing anger through a jawbone that was tightly clenched, as the memories flooded back.

"No." was the reply eventually.

"Are you sure?"

"I am sure."

Toni walked back through the door with the coffees. She picked up the tension Giovanni's face.

"Are you Ok Gio?"

"Yes very well, DI Ball has been very helpful."

Jonty passed his condolences to Toni as he drank his coffee, wished them both well, and left.

CHAPTER TWO

BOONE COUNTY. IOWA.

December 4th, 1997

 Jake and Emily Hughes were in the Christmas mood. They were back in Boone after staying in Manchester, England, to help DI Jonty Ball research and identify the murder of Paul Jennings twenty-four years earlier.
 Jake encountered visions from a previous life following a chance meeting with Billy Jones. The meeting gave him a strong feeling he had been Jennings in a previous life, he slowly convinced Ball that this appeared true as several regressions brought out facts that Jake could not have known.
 Today, Jake and Em were in south story street, Des-Moines, in between Herman Park and cedar pointe golf course hunting down a large Christmas tree for the lounge. Em missed home so much after the six months unplanned stay in England. The snow was fluttering down and just beginning to settle.
 Em was feeling very excited she was in her home county looking at her favourite tree. A white pine, grown in Iowa, she loved the fluffy and the very soft to the touch feel of this tree. It has needles longer than the Scotch Pine, usually 2 to 3 inches in length, better for decoration hanging. She felt the full look looked more 'Christmassy' than the others. Jake, as usual, let her choose the one she wanted. They had been in Scotson's tree yard for over an hour

whilst Em finally decided it was between two. It was now which one of the two.

Em had been happily humming Christmas songs, ranging from 'God rest ye merry gentlemen' to 'the most wonderful time of the year.' and everything in between! It was only the fourth of December but Em loved an early Christmas house. Jake was happy to see her settled, after all, she had been through in England. A horrific car chase had made her physically sick in the hire car they drove, they were chased through the streets of Manchester by gangsters in a Range Rover. If it wasn't for the old gentleman who strode purposefully into the road with a rifle and shot their pursuers they would probably be dead by now. Jake shuddered as he thought about it, then smiled as his lovely wife continued humming, her latest was the Nat King Cole Christmas song, she was now physically singing.

"Chestnuts roasting on an open fire, Jack Frost nipping at your nose." she sang loud enough to make other shoppers smile. She dressed in snow boots with jeans tucked inside them with a red duffle coat and a red woolen hat with a white scarf separating the two! A pair of red and white mittens completed the look. The weather was much colder than normal for December and the freak weather had brought the fluttering of snow. Em was in her element.

"While you decide between the last two, I will go and look for some logs for the fire," Jake told Em.

"Ok I think I know which one I want I will see you in two minutes," she replied.

Jake made his way to another side of the yard looking for wood to buy for the log burner, he would normally collect the wood through the summer but because of the stay in

England, he would have to buy wood late this year. He began looking through the different types of kiln-dried wood and reading which would be best from the short A4 definitions of each type next to the wood, finally deciding on ash to burn along with a cherry to generate a nice smell for the holidays.

He had been looking at the logs for around ten minutes when he thought to himself, '*I wonder where Em got to she said she would only be two minutes.*'

He walked around the yard, he could not see her, he went back to where the two trees were, both were knocked down. Lay on the floor was one of the mittens Em had been wearing. Jake froze before turning to the office inside the store and raced to the cashier.

"Who is in charge here?" Jake demanded to the young man working on the counter.

"Can I help sir?" He asked.

"No said Jake, I need the supervisor and I need him now. My wife has gone missing!"

John Riley, the store manager strolled over. "Can I help you sir?" he asked Jake.

"Yes my wife was here looking at trees she has now disappeared, the trees have been knocked over and one of the mittens she was wearing has been left on the floor, the sign of a struggle is showing in the snow."

"Let me see Sir," Riley replied.

"Forget the look, do you have CCTV?" Jake shouted.

"Yes sir, but…"

"But nothing!" Jake replied, "Let's look now!"

Riley looked at Jake and could see the urgency in his face.

"Come with me," he said to Jake, "Bobby call the police." He told the man on the counter.

They went into an office off the hallway only yards away from the counter area. Riley set the CCTV where the trees were set and rolled it back thirty minutes, Jake saw Em looking at the trees on the screen, he watched with Riley as two men with scarves wrapped around their mouths and large hats. They approached her from behind. One man put his arm around Em as she instantly struggled the man placed gauze around her mouth, she slumped instantly.

"Chloroform!" Jake shouted.

The second man placed a large wheelbarrow behind her as the attacker who had Em in his arms dropped her into the wheelbarrow, the second man placed sacking over her motionless body to hide her from view, they wheeled her outside the gates of the store.

"Do you have a camera outside the gates?" Jake shouted at Riley.

Riley was already on the case, he swapped the cameras to the outside gates. They saw the men push the barrow to the back of a Mercedes SUV, open the tailgate and lift her in the boot. The number plate blanked off by the Men, probably anticipating the use of the CCTV!

As the CCTV gave up the last pictures two 1997 Chevrolet Corvette Police Cars sped to the store with sirens breaking the relaxing Christmas music being fed through the Company piping system.

Sheriff John Smith came into the office, took a statement from Jake and looked through the CCTV again!

"What are you going to do?" Jake asked.

"I will take the footage away and look carefully for any signs that may help."

"Whilst in the meantime we don't know what is happening with my wife!" Jake told the sheriff before adding sarcastically. "Enjoy your coffee while you browse."

Jake stormed out his stomach felt it had been rotated fully inside him, his throat had gone dry and he was aware of a tremble in his hands, not visible as he looked down at them.

"What are you telling me, Jake. People do not get kidnapped in broad daylight without good reason." Christopher Connaught shouted, Christopher was Em's father, as Jake tried explaining to him, and Rachael, Em's Mom, what had happened.

Rachael dressed in a trademark mohair jacket and skirt, an expensive-looking suit with a white cream blouse beneath pressed and fitted under the jacket, her dyed chestnut brown hair made her look fifteen years younger than her age of forty-five. Opposite to Christopher who, though always smart always appeared to keep his grey hair unkempt and collar length, more what you would expect from a university tutor than a top-end high earning attorney.

"This is all attached to what happened in England." Christopher continued.

A deep feeling of nausea swept across Jake as the guilt increased, he knew deep down that Christopher was probably correct Jake excused himself and went to the bathroom where he was physically sick in the fully marbled bathroom that was only a small part of the luxurious house that smelt of wealth. The wealth Christopher had built over the years.

Jake came back down Christopher and Rachael had heard the heaving and belching coming from the bathroom.

"Christopher, Jake loves Emily so much that last thing he needs now is a telling down from you, we want to get Emily back not push Jake away from us," Rachael told him.

"I know we are all shocked, we need to calm down and make sense of this," Christopher replied.

Jake came down the stairs, the trembling was now visible, he could feel his legs shaking violently almost as if he was to fall over like a drunken old man making his way home from the pub.

"I am sorry, you are correct Mr. Connaught," he said as he lowered himself into the grey goat leather armchair that commanded a panoramic view over the stunning Boone countryside. "It probably is an overflow from what happened in Manchester."

Rachael lowered a pot of coffee with a sugar bowl next to it with a plate of biscuits at the side "try and get some sugar inside you, it will help." She told Jake.

They sat in silence for a few moments trying to take in what had happened.

"What are the police doing?" Christopher asked, "Who is dealing with it?"

"Sheriff Smith!" Jake replied.

"I thought he may be. He is good for fender benders and old ladies arguing in the street over car park spaces, but he has not got the experience here, we need a higher level looking at it, the F.B.I. maybe?" Christopher said before adding, "Expense will not be an issue in getting Emily back."

"I think the FBI would be good but I know the best man for the job if we can get him."

"Who would that be?" Christopher asked.

"Jonty Ball, he lead the case in England so will already have a head start on anybody else and he works quickly. I trust him." Jake said.

"Will he work over here to help us?" Rachael asked.

"I am not sure I will need to ask him I guess," Jake said as he took a cup of coffee to clear the taste of vomit in his throat.

The phone rang to break the silence. "Who can that be?" Christopher questioned as he picked the phone up "Christopher Connaught." he answered into the phone as he nestled it against the side of his face.

"Mr. Connaught, You don't know me but your Daughter and son in law have cost me a lot of money with their antics in England."

"Who is this?" demanded Christopher.

The voice laughed "Let me think should I tell you who I am because you have asked?" the voice laughed again. "No, I think I will pass on that question if that's ok with you."

Christopher turned red with rage. "Who is this what do you want?"

"As I said I think I will pass on the, who am I? Part of the question but as you have asked what I want I am happy to oblige with that part of the question."

Christopher went quiet, Jake and Rachael were staring at him they both knew the voice on the other end of the phone was the voice connected to Em's kidnapping.

"First of all, let me clear the air, I do not want ransom money." said the voice.

"Then what do you want?" Christopher bellowed

"I like to call it compensation for the money lost by myself because of the actions of your daughter and son in law."

"Get to the point!" Christopher snarled.

"Two million dollars, no interest charged at this point."

"Are you stupid man, I don't have that amount of money available!"

"Then you are in the wrong industry, Christopher."

The phone went dead.

Christopher relayed the conversation back to Rachael and Jake before looking at Jake square in the eye. "Get Ball over here, I will pay him whatever he asks."

CHAPTER THREE

December 3rd, 1997

The courtroom fell silent in anticipation of the closing statements from both the prosecuting and defence lawyers. There were no spare seats to be found anywhere in the room, the steps outside, like football terraces filled to the brim for a local derby match.

This was no ordinary case. The man on trial was ex-detective James Shepherd accused of being on the payroll of Roberto Sartori, a man who had died of old age after setting up a crime family with his brother Giovanni and Benni Rossi, a New York Mafia boss in the nineteen twenties prohibition era. They found a niche in the bootlegging market transporting top Irish and Scottish whiskey to New York clubs, owned by Rossi, and selling at premium prices.

As the decades passed the three men successfully managed their way through Prohibition and into UK extortion from the coal mining industry until the National Coal Board nationalised the industry on January the first nineteen forty-seven. The men then took advantage of the recent end of World War II buying a munitions factory in 1943, Browns engineering, building a network of crime associates selling rifles to any country in a civil war, or any other conflict with no bias. They sold their new manufactured weapons to either side of any conflict and often both! The business was running profitably until exposed by Detective Jonty Ball in the nineties.

Ball followed a hunch after meeting Jake Hughes who believed he was a reincarnation of Paul Jennings, murdered on the Manchester streets in nineteen seventy-seven. This reincarnation took Ball from a total non-believer to a sceptic and finally a believer with Hughes regressing under a very skillful doctor bringing information to the fore that ignited the death of Paul Jennings moving from accidental death to murder in the space of six months.

The Sartori's and Rossi built the business in England copying the American mafia template. They were money laundering income and expenditure whilst building a team of people in influential places and adding them to the payroll. When Jonty Ball first heard this was happening he dismissed it.

"The mafia well and truly belonged in America and not England!" He had stated.

This was the reason James 'Shep' Shepherd was standing in the dock today waiting for the closing statements and finally the verdict for accused of assisting the Sartori family and its' wide-ranging areas of murder, manipulation, and extortion.

Neil Wynne from Hampshire and Turner Legal practice had represented Shepherd throughout the proceedings but had to pass to a Barrister called Mervyn Brookes. The case was too complicated for Wynne.

Brookes was a seasoned pro at this type of trial, although he had never represented a police officer accused of working for the underworld before this case.

Brookes stood up, he was mid-forties and at the top of his game and he looked it. He was dressed in a Saville row suit that was navy with a narrow grey pinstripe. It made him look taller than his already imposing six-foot four-inch frame. He wore highly black polished leather shoes on which could be mistaken for thinking a face could be reflected in them. His crisp starched white cotton shirt was framed by collar length salt and pepper hair that sat on top of his collar, it had a natural wave in it that gave him the nickname of 'Rich' because he resembled Richard Gere, the film star. This was finished off with a navy tie clamped by a sparkling solid silver bar keeping it pressed in place against his well-trained chest.

He took one final look at his notes bound in a soft tan coloured leather casing that oozed wealth and a man not to oppose in his territory of a courtroom.

"Ladies and Gentlemen of the Jury, I am as you are all aware here to represent my client, Detective Inspector James Shepherd, Who is I believe, still a detective inspector unless proven guilty by you, the jury, when delivering your final verdict!" he paused hoping this would plant some authority in their minds.

"DI Shepherd has been a good honest working police officer for thirty years protecting you all and your families along with myself and my family from a host of unsavory characters on our streets. He has done this because of his love of the law and his belief that normal family life is important to him."

He pointed at Shepherd who sat motionless dressed in a smart navy suit, light blue shirt, and red tie. His face was clean-shaven with a few red patches around his chin, giving the impression that the last shave he had was to take a beard or days of stubble away. His eyes were soulless and his demeanor forlorn, a resigned fifty-something-man who had given up on the justice system.

"This man has been accused of implication to murder and perverting the cause of justice whilst being on the payroll of a crime family waiting for orders to act! The case cannot be fully satisfied surely without the evidence of Superintendent John Quinn."

He looked over at Jonty Ball and continued, "DI Ball has worked tirelessly in raising this case and placing it in front of you, however, there are surely some discrepancies in his case."

Jonty sat on the seat watching proceedings wearing a black suit, white shirt, and black and white striped shirt on. His hands were clasped tight between his slightly opened legs, the knuckles had turned white with the force of clamping them together. His hands were sweating and he could feel beads developing on his forehead even though the courtroom was not hot.

'This case has to be won for so many people!' he thought,

It was an accumulation from the death of Paul Jennings who had been murdered twenty years earlier to Paul's mother, Helen Jennings, who had developed a loving relationship with Jonty and they were due to be married in a month.

He thought of Jake Hughes the American he first thought of as a freak because he thought he was Paul Jennings reincarnated. Jake and his wife, Emily, escaped a murder attempt by the men Shepherd was supporting!

Brookes continued. "As you may be aware, Superintendent Quinn was an accessory in assisting the escape of the leader of this crime outfit, William Jones, they both escaped into thin air, perhaps DI Ball just wants to end the reams of paperwork built up on the case so he can close it and get on with something else."

"Objection, My Lord!" Bellowed a voice from the corner of the room.

Barrister Samuel Price was acting on behalf of the prosecuting service. He had worked complicated cases for the crown many times before. Now in his early sixties, he had an arthritic hip that showed badly when he rose from a chair but eased after a few steps, his hair was white with ruddy cheeks and a veined nose linked to an excess of fine red wine both he and his wife, Prudence, had become accustomed to over the years. He had a double chin that flapped over a white-collar which appeared too tight around his large neck. His stomach hung over his waistband and the look finished off by what looked like thin stick-like legs. Appearances could be false. Price was renowned in the legal circles like a lion amongst men.

"Sustained!" Judge Beckett agreed, sat in his seat with his red robes on whilst wearing his aged wig that always added to the visual thought relating to his undoubted experience. "Wipe that from the records!" he continued.

"Apologies to the court, and the Jurors." Brookes continued, however, the reason for the comment was to plant a seed in the Juror's minds not to make a statement!

"The point I am making is, without the evidence of Superintendent Quinn. The case must be made inadmissible, as he was the manager of both DI's Shepherd and Ball." he paused again and looked for some reaction from the Jury, a nod here or a nod there to relay to him that he was making a forward move, none came.

"And if you agree with me, as you surely must?"

"Objection!"

"Sustained!"

"And if you agree with me. Then surely, there are grounds for unreasonable doubt to find this hard-working pillar of society guilty. You will hear from the prosecuting side how it was all about money, and I agree he did take money, but it was never on the premise that he would be involved in murder or corruption. If you can see there are grounds of unreasonable doubt then the law asks you to find my client, NOT GUILTY!"

He thanked the Jury for their time, went back to his desk, and sat down smiling at his team of four, who all sat behind him.

"Prosecution do you have a closing statement?" Judge Beckett asked.

"Yes My Lord." Price answered in his plummy deep husky voice that matured following years of smoking the best Havana cigars.

"Members of the Jury," he opened, "I sat with enthusiastic interest listening to the closing statement of the defence, as, I am sure you did," He looked at the Jury and made a slight nod to several of them with an impromptu nod coming back to him, a trick learned years ago.

"I had real problems understanding why we have to receive the views of Superintendent Quinn. In fact if he were here today he would be sat where Mr. Shepherd sits today as the accused surely." he paused to let the words sink in before continuing.

"Let us consider what Superintendent Quinn did, he flew a helicopter into the grounds of William Jones, the leader of a crime family, who in his own right would be accused of murder today."

"Objection My Lord, you cannot bring accusations into a closing speech, surely Superintendent Quinn and William Jones are innocent until otherwise proven guilty!" it was Brookes turn to counter.

"Sustained!" was the Judge's response.

"There is no doubt that at this point Quinn would be on trial but there is no getting away that he flew in a helicopter and assisted Jones allegedly escaping in a Lear Jet over the Irish Sea." He let the Jury consider for another few seconds.

"Regarding DI Shepherd there is clear evidence of obstructing an inquiry by shredding a statement from Aston Police regarding the black stolen BMW, that eventually killed Paul Jennings!"

"Objection! My Lord, there is no evidence of Mister Shepherd shredding any such document. We only have evidence of the paper being faxed from Aston Police Station."

"Sustained!"

Jonty began to feel defeat in his stomach, Shepherd was guilty and everybody knew it *Price needs to hit a point that cannot be challenged* he thought.

"Let me take you to another point that came up earlier in the proceedings, that of DI Shepherd assisting in hiding vital evidence. He blatantly hid HGV side covers with the name 'VERDE' showing on the side, this HGV was involved in gun-running, and the theft of an automobile, which was also caught on camera by DI Ball." He nodded towards Jonty, the jury followed his nod and all looked at Jonty with him.

"What of the confession whereby DI Shepherd admitted being present at DI David Rowlands home, he admitting picking foxglove flowers to assist Quinn in murder, a plan plotted in the knowledge that these poisonous flowers can kill people with a weak heart, as DI Rowlands did."

"Objection! Quinn is not on trial here, and should he be in the future, he will be innocent until proved guilty!" shouted Brookes.

"Sustained! Mister Price, please do not accuse people wrongly, FINAL WARNING!"

"Sorry, My Lord."

Price continued, "If the side covers to the HGV are factual, which they are," he stopped and looked at

Brookes, who put his head down as he could not challenge factual evidence." The jury looked at Brookes in unison.

"Added, to the fact that DI Shepherd was on the pay list of a money-laundering account from an illegal bank account." again he looked at Brookes who was still looking at the ground showing no response.

"Finally." Price continued, lowering his aged husky voice. "DI Shepherd was a police officer receiving a salary paid for, by you and me, the taxpayer." The jury made unintended nods. "His contract clearly states that if he is to receive any additional income he must have this agreed by his superiors." the jury was now listening intently as Price continued.

"His immediate line manager, Superintendent John Quinn, was also on the payroll of Roberto Sartori. Along with the man he shared the helicopter journey with, William Jones." Price was careful to close this out with 'shared a journey,' and including using the word, **'with'**, as this was also a fact, Brookes could not challenge.

Price thanked the jury and asked them, "Please make the decision your conscience feels is correct following the evidence brought before you in this trial."

The following day the jury sat in front of a packed courtroom again, the press could not have enough column space or airtime on the case that had gripped the nation for the last two weeks.

The Foreman stood up, Judge Beckett asked, "Have you arrived at a decision?"

"We have, My Lord," replied Foreman Foster an electrician by trade, with a small local company.

"And what is your decision on assisting murder?"

"Not guilty My Lord."

"And your decision on perverting the course of justice?"

"Guilty my lord."

Shepherd's head dropped, he was expecting the guilty verdict but it was too early to think how lucky he was to escape the murder plea.

'*Bingo!*' Jonty thought! He walked over and shook Price's hand "Well done." he said.

Shepherd was sentenced to ten years in jail, where he knew his cellmates would have a field day sharing a cell with a bent copper.

CHAPTER FOUR.

Manchester December 4th, 1997

"This kidnapping has implications on everything that went on a few months ago Sir," Jonty said to Superintendent Ron Morris.

Morris had been offered the position in the wake of his predecessor Superintendent John Quinn, who whilst being on the Greater Manchester Police payroll as a Superintendent he was also on the payroll of Britain's largest crime family, headed by Roberto Sartori.

Quinn's role was to manage a team of police officers who took money every month from the crime family in return for their services in any specialist area they may have. Jonty had exposed one, his old working colleague James Shepherd, Jonty knew there were more but he could not identify them.

Finding Quinn could take this forward but Quinn had rescued his crime boss Billy Jones, who was the grandson of Roberto Sartori, he had been given the role of the godfather, as Roberto aged beyond the position, the capture of Jones seemed inevitable as he was surrounded and penned into his own home. A daring plan by Quinn had seen him book a police helicopter and appeared to be taking Jones and his wife, Maggie, as prisoners when, he, hired a jet to transport the three of them to a Country yet to be identified by Jonty.

Morris had been in the GMP force for twenty-five years of which the last five were as a Superintendent, Jonty didn't know much of Morris as the majority of his career had been gained in the Bristol area, a fact that was proved each time he spoke in his southwest 'country' voice.

Morris was six foot two and built strongly with short grey hair and piercing blue eyes, he had very strong bone structure particularly on the jawline with a square chin that earned him the nickname of Superman after the comic hero Clarke Kent. His Lois Lane was Joanne who he met from the force in Bristol when he was in his mid-twenties working his way through to Detective Inspector.

"We have an ex-superintendent who went AWOL whilst helping a dangerous crime suspect, who I might add, was cornered by crack firearms specialists, to escape from under our noses." Jonty continued.

"Billy Jones was a man who dealt with some of the toughest and unforgiving men on this planet, and as a result of me closing down a bank account that was used for paying off these men and other associates from laundered money. A girl, who I got to know very well has been kidnapped and is being held for ransom as we speak."

"It's the cost of the operation Jonty, we have no budget, Let the FBI deal with it!" Morris said.

"The cost is nothing compared with the life of a person, and linked in this somewhere is ex-Superintendent Quinn who fled and is living it up somewhere and nobody has a clue of his whereabouts. This crime is deep and touches places you could not even dream of." Jonty, paused before continuing,

"I am going sir, regardless of you agreeing or not, I would like to go officially to support the FBI but if not I will go solo," Jonty said with authority.

"That could cost you your Job Jonty."

"But not my dignity and conscience." was the instant reply.

Jake called Jonty from Christopher's house within a minute of Christopher telling him to 'get Ball.' Jonty also wanting to get things moving was in Morris's office within fifteen minutes of the phone call, it was the end of the day UK time. Jonty would have been in sooner but his second task was to book a flight to Des-Moines. His first task was to call Helen his wife.

"Jonty how is she?" Helen asked.

"I don't know any more than I have told you, but if you are OK with me flying to the USA I will book a flight and see Morris," Jonty told her.

"Do it, get there as quick as you can," replied Helen who had seen Jake and Em as children she never had, after a rocky start with them she had grown to love them dearly, and in return they loved her.

The flight was booked for nine forty-five the following morning leaving from Manchester and flying to Stockholm where a three-hour wait would see him board a flight to O'Hare International in Chicago before the final leg taking him to Des Moines, Iowa. Jake agreed to pick him up. The total time travelling would be twenty-one hours. That would mean he would be touching down at around midnight the following day local time as they are six hours behind London.

Jonty received a call from Morris at eight in the evening to tell him the Chief Superintendent had agreed to it, as nothing was more important to the Chief Inspector that catching his ex-Superintendent John Quinn.

The flights were long and boring but nothing out of the ordinary, Jonty watched movies, one was Jaws which he endured for the fifth time! He enjoyed a James Bond film,

Goldfinger, with Sean Connery as the lead, '*Always the best Bond in my book.*' he thought, but he did enjoy all Bond films and had seen everyone made.

The food made his stomach feel bunged up, 'There is only so much airplane food you can take before getting stomach cramps! He laid off the booze on the flight as he knew the jet lag would be bad enough, he did not need anything else to fuel it!'

Finally, he landed in Des-Moines where he picked up the luggage Helen had packed for him, negotiated customs, and saw a weary friendly face. Jake!

They walked out of the airport, the weather was cool without being over cold, a light smattering of snow was blustering in the night air which was hard to tell if it was coming from the sky or just being churned around in the breeze.

"I am so glad you could make it Jonty," Jake said, first shaking his hand and then reaching out to hug him before finally helping him carry his luggage.

"The circumstances are not the best to meet again, but I want to help Em all I can," he told Jake. "Helen sends every ounce of love for you too."

Jake smiled and replied, "I love her too."

The journey took fifty minutes from the airport to Jake and Em's four-bedroom house in Woodland Avenue. Woodland Avenue is in a sought after area of Des-Moines. It has a very low crime rate, the streets are tree-lined down the length of them with grass fringes of about six feet either side of the road. There are two-foot-wide footpaths with further grass leading to the gardens of each house, even though it was winter and past midnight, Jonty could tell it was a nice area.

They entered the four-bed two-bathroom house that was tastefully decorated, Jonty could see Em's influence in the pastel colour's a lovely pastel green covering the lounge walls were complemented by oak flooring and a cream leather modern three piece suite sat around an oak coffee table in the middle of the floor matching the floor colour perfectly.

Jake led Jonty up the stairs and opened a brilliant white painted door that led into a modern, decorated double bedroom with an inviting double bed covered in pastel, and a blue duvet to match the pastel blue walls. Jonty smiled and looked at it, like a man who had crossed a desert with no water, and was sighting it for the first time in days.

"You need some sleep, it's great you're here, see you in the morning!" Jake said.

"God that bed looks a sight for sore eyes." Jonty said as he dragged his aching bones over the cream carpet towards heaven, in the shape of a bed.

Jake walked to his bedroom. He had not slept for two days, he knew his brain was not functioning correctly through the lack of sleep. He showered and climbed into his bed he felt warm and comforted, he knew that Sheriff Smith had not advanced the case in the two days since EM's abduction but he felt comfort knowing Jonty was here, *it would speed up now,* he thought.

CHAPTER FIVE

Des-Moines December 5th, 1997

Jonty woke up the following morning not feeling fully refreshed, he felt another few hours would clear the jet lag still running through his veins but the important thing was to get onto the case and find the people who had kidnapped Em, his own trivial jet lag problem would clear in a day or two. It was nine in the morning and therefore three in the afternoon in Manchester, his first job was to call Helen and let her know he was safe and he was with Jake at their home.

Jonty came downstairs to see Jake, preparing their breakfast.

"Em is the cook in the house so you will have to make do with my cooking," Jake said.

"Well, I could certainly do with a good breakfast after the food on the plane." Jonty replied, "What are we having?"

"Florentine Breakfast Pizza."

"Never heard of it," Jonty told him.

"It's crescent rolls, chopped spinach, thawed I think" Jake joked as he continued, "6 slices of bacon, shredded Mozzarella, eggs, milk, mustard and pepper" he finished as he placed a huge plate under Jonty's nose.

"I just love a heart attack on a plate," he said.

"I know I saw you eat a double English breakfast, don't forget," Jake said with a laugh.

"Ok, you win," Jonty said taking his first forkful.

"Are you not eating?" Jonty asked Jake.

"I have no appetite, I just want to get cracking at finding Em, You know you love somebody but you don't know how much until something happens that separates you."

"I know but we will get cracking on this today," Jonty replied, feeling a little guilty that he had a huge appetite in a situation like this whilst Jake just drank fresh orange juice.

They finished breakfast and hit the road by nine forty-five, first stop, the sheriff's office.

Sheriff John Smith sat at his desk with a large coffee perched in front of him. This made Jake instantly annoyed, *'Why are they drinking coffee and not looking for Em.'* he thought.

"Morning Gentlemen how can I help?" he said with a stern face.

Jake was now feeling his blood boil, Smith spoke as if he could not remember him.

"I have come to see if there is any progress on the search for my wife?" Jake said.

"Nothing yet, we will let you know as soon as we find anything out."

"You need to work on this and work on it now!" Jake shouted.

"Hang on a minute boy, I am the Sheriff around here and I will say what, and when things get done, do you understand?"

"No, I don't understand!" Jake fired back at him. "I need help finding her and I want it now!"

Sheriff Smith was around fifty and had let the weight take over from what was once a fit agile body, his sand coloured shirt was bursting at the buttons showing that it probably fit when he first received the uniform but he had outgrown it! On the arm of the shirt was his sheriff badge a brown semi-circular badge to the top with two forty-five degree angles coming off towards a straight bottom line. There was gold braiding within the badge and the words Boone County wrote in the semi-circle shape at the top, with Sheriff written in a straight line towards the bottom. In the middle was a gold star with the letters IOWA emblazoned in dark brown.

"And you are?" he looked at Jonty.

"You don't need to know who I am." Jonty told Smith then turned to Jake. "Come on Jake we need to start work."

They sat in Jakes Volvo Amazon, a car made in the sixties, the car was in pristine condition. It was Jake's pride and joy, it always turned heads and its racing green colour and beige leather seats with column control gears made it stand out in any crowd.

Jonty told Jake he was going to make a wild card decision. He called Ros, short for Rosalyn, at the station, Quinn's ex-Personal assistant, and now Morris's

"Jonty it's so good to hear your voice, was the trip OK?"

"Yes thanks, Ros, I need you to do me a favour can you get me a telephone number, you may have to search a little for it?"

Jonty and Jake left the Sheriff's office and travelled back to Jake's office, agreed it would be better to be in a working environment than Jake's lounge.

As he walked in all the staff greeted Jake but nobody asked any questions. It felt like there was an unwritten rule not to ask.

Jonty and Jake had been in the office for less than five minutes when Jake's manager. Ron Rodgers walked in. Rogers was a hardnosed hard-hitting executive. He had been Jake's direct line since his promotion two years earlier. He never liked Jake, one night at the Company Christmas party, Rodgers picked a fight with Jake outside when nobody was around, meaning there would be no evidence, he wanted to hurt Jake in a fistfight, He would have no problem beating 'laid back' Jake, Ron after all regularly did weights, had a six-pack that he showed at any opportunity. He could easily bench press two hundred pounds. Jake would be spending Christmas 1997 in hospital, right? Wrong! He swung a punch at Jake. Jake dropped his left shoulder allowing the swing to go over his head. Ron lost a little balance, Jake scythed his leg across Ron's calf, this toppled Ron, a normal strength person would have fallen to the ground but Ron's strength allowed him to keep on his feet, within a split second a roundhouse kick caught Ron on the jaw. The crunch of bone was deafening then in the same move, a punch came directly down the line contacted Ron's nose which spread over his face like a balloon full of water being dropped on a six-inch nail. Ron was unsteady, Jake thrust one final kick to the ribs and a final knee to the already disjointed nose as he was bending from the last hit. Ron collapsed like a bag of coal dropping down a cellar. Nobody told Ron that the new member of his team had accrued a black belt in karate over years of hard physical training. This did nothing to adhere Jake to Ron.

When Jake was initially in England with Em. They went to enjoy a walking vacation, walking Wainwright's famous Coast to Coast walk, A chance meeting, with Billy Jones and his wife Maggie, in a hotel bar one evening, convinced Jake that he had been Paul Jennings in a previous life, following things said in conversation and linking them to recurring dreams Jake had as a child. This resulted in him helping Jonty discover the Sartori family and their hidden life of crime.

Jake rang Ron to ask for an extension of his holiday in England as he needed to prove to himself that he was Jennings reincarnated, although this was not the reason gave Rogers.

"I'll tell you what Jake, I will give you two weeks further vacation, unpaid, then you can look for another job do you understand that?" Was Rogers' response however mainly because of the sixty years the Sartori family had been operating undetected and the dramatic escape by Quinn and Jones, it had hit the media on both sides of the Atlantic. The board agreed that keeping Jake on was good not only as a good employee but the fact that he was their employee and there was god PR to be seen in it.

"Jake I am so sorry to hear about Em, I won't keep you but if there is anything I can do to help please let me know!" Rogers said, nodding at Jonty, Jonty nodded back with a straight face, he was aware of the conversation in England.

"Use the office as often as you need to, feel free anything we can do to help." The original sincerity appeared to be changing a little the more he spoke!

"Thanks, Ron, this is Detective Inspector Jonty Ball from England."

"Good to meet you Jonty, you look different in the flesh than on a TV screen." with that Rogers left the office.

Jake never told anybody except Em that Ron had told everybody he fell off his motorbike after getting a blowout after the fight, he couldn't face the truth.

Ron left just as Jonty's phone rang. "Hi Jonty it's Ros, I found the number and I have the person on the phone would you like to speak to him now?"

"Ros you are a star what would that station do without you? Yes please put him through." Ros felt warm and wanted, Jonty and Ros always got on well, he made her feel valued, the payback was she would do the extra mile to help, as she was now.

"I am putting you through now Mr. Sartori." These were the final words Jonty heard from Ros as the phone clicked.

"Mr. Sartori, thanks for taking the time to chat to me, I have Jake Hughes with me, would you mind if I put the conversation on to hands-free?"

"Not at all and it's Giovanni." was the reply "How can I help?"

"The first thing I should ask is how are the legs after the shooting?" Jonty asked as Jake's eyes lifted in surprise.

"All the metal is out now and my legs are bandaged I can walk with the aid sticks."

"That's progress then," Jonty replied, before continuing to tell Giovanni about the abduction of Em whilst Jake filled in the details where he could.

"I am not sure who did it." Giovanni replied "I would like to know because I have a score to settle with the people who came to Roberto's funeral uninvited." referring to the helicopter that killed the Archbishop and wounded him. "I am willing to bet it's the same people!"

Jonty agreed.

"Let me do some homework and I will get back to you!" Giovanni replied. Then the phone went dead.

Three in the afternoon came and went as Jonty's phone rang again.

"Jonty its Giovanni, If I give you a number to call I think they can help you but you must not take any actions against the people if you see or hear anything."

"Agreed." Jonty said, "I just want Em's safe return."

"Talk to Gino Abano he is the new head of the Rossi Family in New York." Giovanni gave Jonty a phone number and the call ended.

"He is short and sweet in conversation," Jake said.

"Yes but highly effective I think," Jonty replied with respect in his voice.

Jonty rang the number Giovanni gave him.

"Ciao." was the reply in a thick Italian accent.

"Good afternoon can I speak to Gino Abano?" Jonty asked

"This is Gino, who is speaking?"

"My name is Jonty Ball, Giovanni asked me to call you."

"Ah Mr. Ball, Giovanni told me to expect a call, he said I may be able to help, I will do all I can, when can you be in New York?"

"Tomorrow?"

"Fantastico I will have one of my men pick you up, let me know your flight details when you have them." the phone went dead

"Vodafone will never make any profits with the amount of time this lot spend on a phone." Jonty Joked.

Jake laughed for the first time in three days. Jonty had only been here a day and it was moving already.

Jake fired up his desktop computer and looked for flights from Des-Moines airport in Boone to New York.

"There is a flight at eight this evening to Newark. It's a four-hour flight we will be there just after midnight. I can book a hotel we will be tucked up in bed by one."

"Go for it we just have enough time to pack," Jonty responded knowing time was of the essence.

CHAPTER SIX

December 5th, 1997

Em was comfortable in the chair she had been placed, the room was large and expensive. Her senses kicked into overdrive. With her eyes, she could see the large room that owned high ceilings along with deep red long velvet curtains that were shut.

'Obviously for security, so I can't get my bearings,' she thought.

Two leather maroon chesterfield sofa's sat facing each other, they were adjacent to a large open fire that housed a two-foot-wide grate in a four-foot-wide inglenook which was also four feet high giving it perfect symmetry. The floor was mid-tan solid mahogany wood, with a large square Persian rug boasting a flower design of red with green and yellow.

Her senses changed from sight to sound, she could hear birds singing outside but no traffic noise.

'Possibly in large grounds or the country,' she thought.

She spent a lot of time in the countryside with Jake, and with her family growing up she rode horses to a good standard. Em, could often be seen in the Ledges Country Park in Boone.

She recognised the sound of the Piping Plover warbling through the window, she could still be in Boone as she knew this was a rare bird that was at risk within the county.

She concentrated on smell, wood was burning in the grate to keep the December chill outside, it smelt sweet and was possibly cherry, no clues there! The remaining smells were of leather being shared in the room from the sofas, matching the club chair she sat in.

She rose and walked to the door, she turned the handle, *'Locked!'*

She looked at the grandfather clock sat at one end of the room which read six-fifteen, her watch concurred.

'Is it morning or evening?' She thought, there was no way of telling with the curtains drawn and not knowing how long she had been unconscious

The door opened, a middle-aged man walked through the door. He wore an expensive-looking Armani style single-breasted suit in dark blue with a crisp white shirt and red tie finished off in what looked like Jimmy Choo style shoes.

"Emily good to meet you." The man said.

"Who are you what do you want?" Em shrieked.

"Calm down said the man." he stroked his chin and smiled, "You and Jake have cost me a lot of money, This is just business, you are safe, as long as your father pays your dues to me."

"How can I have cost you so much money?" Em shouted not calming down from her original shriek.

"Well Emily, let me spell it out to you." He sat down on one of the sofa's about six feet away.

"I am being a terrible host, can I offer you a drink after your journey?" he smugly smiled with the words.

"I am not thirsty?" Shrilled Em "Let me go before it gets worse for you!"

The man's smile turned into a laugh "Let me know if you get thirsty," he continued "I will be calling your father in a few minutes again."

"Again?"

"Yes Emily again, we have already discussed payment for my compensation regarding the costs owed to me by Green's Engineering in England."

Em knew a little about it from discussions with Jonty and Jake, but the infinite details were not familiar.

"Green's Engineering?" she asked.

"Yes Emily, because of the interference of Jonty Ball and your husband, Jake, The bank accused Green's Engineering of money laundering freezing their accounts. Owing me, and my partners two million pounds." He looked at Em with steel now in his already black eyes.

The man spoke with a European accent that Em could not place.

He picked up his mobile phone and punched in the numbers.

"Christopher I have your Daughter Emily with me, she has had a lovely sleep," He said with a chuckle in his throat.

"If you do anything to her I will make sure you are killed!" Christopher shouted.

"Now! Now! Christopher I am surely the one holding all the cards, think about it." the man waited a few seconds to add more impact. "I have Emily, you don't. I know where she is you don't. I can harm her you can't save her. I know who you are. You don't know who I am." all went silent again.

"I think that leaves me in the driving seat Christopher don't you?" Christopher never answered.

"I thought we would agree. How is your collection of my money progressing? Well, I presume?"

"I have started the ball rolling, it will take at least two weeks to get that amount of money together."

"I am an understanding man Christopher, I am a businessman Christopher, I know it will take time. You have until the 19th December if you want to see your daughter, then we will review our situation," he said with no threat but the definite menace in his voice.

The nineteenth was selected because Billy had to pay his debt by the end of December, it allowed two weeks to open to get things organised.

The man put the phone down and turned to Em, "You are with me for a further two weeks Emily that is a long time to get to know each other, let us start with a nice meal. What can I get you?"

"Go to hell!" Em shouted at the top of her voice.

"Well maybe I will go to hell in the future, but for now I will go to my lounge," He left the room and Em alone again.

Christopher rang Jonty at the first opportunity and relayed the conversation to him.

"That's good Christopher it gives us a week to set up a strategy and find Em," Jonty replied not wanting to say it could be drastic action such as the classic taking a finger or ear off for each day Christopher misses a payment.

After the conversation, Jake said to Jonty. "Right I am packed for a few days, let's get the plane to JFK."

Jake and Jonty were at Harrison Airport with time to spare, the Volvo sat in the car park and the flight information board showed their flight to be on time.

The Journey was straight forward a change at Chicago from Des Moines to complete the journey to Newark in New Jersey. The plane landed at Newark at 12.15 am, by 12.45 they reached the terminal where they saw a sign with 'Ball' written on it. Holding the board was a man as big as a house at least six foot ten inches and built with muscles that made his arms look like legs protruding from his side, a point Jonty made!

"I'm not telling him that." Jake joked.

"Jonty Ball," Jonty said looking up at the man mountain.

"Pleased to meet you, Mister Ball, My name is Gus." said the man in a strong Bronx accent. The Man took them to the black Lincoln Navigator SUV. The car had privacy windows and nineteen-inch alloy wheels, Gus sat in the front passenger seat whilst the driver opened the rear doors for Jake and Jonty he then entered the driver's seat and smoothly pulled away. The glass private screen, between the front seats and the rear seats, meant no more conversation with Gus or his driver could be made. Jake and Jonty sat contemplating for the hour and ten-minute drive to reach the Quin Hotel on Central Park Way just over the Lincoln Bridge, booked as the cheapest available when Jake used a search engine to find a room.

The SUV pulled against the sidewalk, the boot opened automatically as Gus left the passenger seat to pick up the two suitcases from the rear, he carried them to the hotel lobby, Jake and Jonty followed.

"It looks like he is carrying two newspapers," Jake said to Jonty referring to the ease Gus was carrying the suitcases.

He dropped the suitcases next to the reception desk and took an envelope out of his inside pocket.

"Mister Abano asked me to give you this it is arrangements to meet with him tomorrow," Gus said handing the letter to Jonty.

"It's been good meeting you both, we will meet again, goodnight." Gus then swiveled on his heels with amazing agility for a man his size, he strode back to the car and disappeared into the night.

Jake and Jonty booked into the hotel, found their rooms and both collapsed into a deep sleep!

CHAPTER SEVEN

MANCHESTER 1937.

A fifteen-year-old Matthew Fitzpatrick had lived in England for two years, His Father moved from Belfast to look for work in the promised land of England. The tensions between the protestant and catholic communities were high. A Catholic family in Northern Ireland would always be considered second class people.

In 1921, two-thirds of all Irish industrial workers were concentrated in the north-east of Ulster. The major heavy industries, such as shipbuilding, engineering, and linen manufacturing, had prospered during WW1. However, demand decreased during the nineteen-twenties and thirties, industrial employment fell throughout the UK because of failure to modernise and falling prices. By the mid-twenties nearly a quarter of the workforce in Northern Ireland were unemployed. Many members of the Catholic and Protestant communities believed it was right to show a preference for employment towards someone on religious or political grounds. Protestants believed this was the best way to maintain their supremacy and protect their constitution. Catholics suffered most from unemployment and poverty and so believed that it was only fair that they would be given preference for employment. However, Catholics still faced some discrimination by Protestants in employment.

The reason offered by unionists for such discrimination was that they viewed Catholics as untrustworthy. They view them as always being disloyal to the Crown and always in pursuit of the Irish republic. This was the Protestant main grievance. The Northern Ireland Government was primarily concerned about the employment of Catholics within the Northern Irish administration. Further discrimination was the requirement of an oath of allegiance to the Northern Irish Government to be taken by those in public employment. This was seen by unionists as a test of Catholic loyalty whereas the nationalist resented this mandatory requirement.

This type of discrimination heightened tensions between Catholics and Protestants which later manifested into riots that occurred in the summer of 1935 in Belfast. Previously in nineteen-thirty three and thirty-four, there had been minor outbursts of sectarian violence but the most significant of these began in nineteen-thirty five.

Disturbances from time to time in Belfast in the twenties and thirties such as the nineteen-thirty five Outdoor Relief riots saw Catholics and Protestants demonstrate (and fight) side by side in protest at the cutting of unemployment assistance. Depressingly often, however, violence would resume the old sectarian pattern.

In 1935, after several months of rising tension, riots broke out during the Orange parades on July 12th. Over the next week, two thousand people, mainly Catholics, were forced from their homes, Catholics were driven out of workplaces and several were killed in sectarian attacks. The majority of the eleven people killed in the riots were Protestants, but most of those forced from their homes and injured were Catholic. James Fitzpatrick, his wife

Hannah, and their thirteen-year-old son, Matthew were a family forced to leave to prize a new life in Manchester.

Matthew saw out his last two years at St Phillip's School in Ancoats, an inner-city suburb of Manchester, within a larger Irish population around Manchester. He left school at the age of fourteen. The thirties are remembered for generating mass unemployment. However, there was already mass unemployment, the economy was struck by depression. By the start of nineteen-thirty three unemployment in Britain was 22.8%. Which meant a job prospect for a fresh-faced Irish fourteen-year-old was impossible.

He had friends who were in the same position and they readily turned to crime. One warm June night whilst in Manchester City centre, Matthew and a few friends were seeing what they could steal with the view to selling it on for coppers at the first opportunity. They saw in front of them a Brand new Crossley motor car, the engine was three litres with a top speed of seventy-five miles per hour whilst having an acceleration speed of zero-fifty in twenty-five seconds. Matthew knew the retail cost of the car, it was seven hundred and ninety-five pounds. An amount He and his friends could only dream of.

On the back seat sat a jewellery box that was closed, it was around six inches long and about two inches wide, definitely a watch or neckless, and judging by the car it was sat in probably expensive too. Matthew looked around and saw a large thick piece of wood, probably used for a robbery earlier in the day and abandoned after the heist was successful, or not!

He took it in his hands and held it baseball style, he took a long measured swing at it and it bounced off the window, he tried again and the sound of breaking glass broke the silence on the streets. Just as the window smashed into small pieces, he heard a voice.

"Hey, you boy what do you think you are doing?"

At the sound of the voice, Matthews friends ran, but Matthew tried to reach in and take the box before he was going to evacuate the scene, he took too long, the man had reached the car and was dragging Matthew out of the car by the scruff of his neck. Matthew knew he could not match the strongly built thirty-something man for strength, he was being lifted off his feet.

"Rose call the police and tell them to get here quickly!"

He need not have bothered he heard a police whistle blow and it was close by, constables on the beat at that time blew whistles alerting other constables in the area to assist.

Matthew had to think quickly, he kept hold of the wooden club he turned and swung it with all his might. He missed. The swing was so hard he lost balance and nearly fell over. The man took a step back knowing he needed to get past the club before he could get to Matthew.

The man bounced up and down on his feet waiting to avoid the next swing which inevitably came, again a miss, the man was seeing the swings coming almost before Matthew was starting his arc.

"What is going on here?" asked the bobby who had now arrived on the scene, the man turned for a split second, Matthew saw his chance the club landed square on the man's cheek. He swung again landing the wood on the man's skull. The man fell to his knees, another swing and it went straight down the middle of his head. The man fell, blood seeping from his ears and head, Matthew stood over him and held the wood in the position of an axeman chopping wood for the winter fire, he felt resistance, the bobby grabbed the wood, Matthew could not swing it down, the strength of an undernourished teenager was no match for a fully-grown man. Within thirty seconds there were three police officers on the scene Matthew tried to resist their efforts but all was in vain. wrestled to the floor, hands tied behind his back, and frog marched to Bootle Street police station.

CHAPTER EIGHT

December 6[th,] 1997

Jonty and Jake were up early, they took an early breakfast of eggs on toast, Jonty fried whilst Jake took a healthier option of scrambled. Jonty reopened the envelope given to him by Gus with the arrangements to meet Abano as they drank a hot strong coffee giving them the caffeine they knew they would require.

"We have to meet Abano at the New York Mandarin Oriental Hotel at 10 AM. Do you know it?" Jonty asked

"Only by reputation, five stars," Jake answered.

They hired a yellow cab for nine promptly as they did not want to be late and knew they needed to get over the morning traffic jams.

"Jake felt his stomach turning over, he wasn't hungry at breakfast but Jonty forced him to eat, he did feel better initially but the breakfast was now feeling heavy.

"What if they can't help us?" Jake asked Jonty, his voice shaking with nerves.

"Let's take each step as it comes," Jonty replied.

The cab snaked its way across the city at a crawl as early commuters were fighting for the same goal of their day's employment.

"Don't worry I will get you there on time." The cab driver said as the clock inched past nine-thirty.

Jake wrung his hands, it was a cold clear December day but Jake was sweating without feeling warm his hands were constantly moving from a horizontal wipe across his mouth to clenched between his knees, a point Jonty had not missed, he put his hand on Jake's knee.

"It will be Ok Jake, we will sort this."

The cab finally turned into Sixtieth Street arrived at the hotel at 80 Columbus Circle with five minutes to spare, Jonty paid the cab driver and took the receipt, *'This will go on expenses,'* Jonty thought.

Jonty shut the taxi door and took a few seconds to take in the surroundings. The hotel was set right at the top of the Time Warner Center, with views over Central Park. *The Mandarin Oriental is pure luxury.* Jonty thought.

It had breathtaking views within walking distance of Fifth Avenue and Broadway.

Jake and Jonty walked to the reception, "We are here to see Mister Abano?" Jonty said to the receptionist who looked in her early thirties, the prime of her life. She wore the hotel uniform which was navy with a red piece added into the front of the blazer, behind her stood a gold fan with gold lettering making you have no doubts where you were, The Mandarin Oriental, New York!

The girl looked at the computer screen to check the name Abano. "Ah, here we are," she said, with the enthusiasm that made her look like she had just invented a cure for hunger in the third world, instead of finding a guest on the hotel computer.

"Mister Abano is in the Oriental Suite on the fifty-fourth floor." she directed them to the lifts and the two friends were on their way. They left the lift and walked to the suite door, they knocked and a known face answered, it was Gus, dressed in a charcoal grey single-breasted suit with a white shirt and a red tie, he looked as menacing as ever. His size dwarfed the doorframe.

"Mister Ball! Mister Hughes! Good to see you again." Gus said with a friendly smile that looked like it could change at will. He stood back to let Jonty and Jake cross the threshold. A man in his early fifties walked over to them.

"I am Gino Abano, it's good to meet you. I trust your journey was good." The man said in an Italian accent.

Jonty and Jake took it in turns to shake the hand of the smiling man, he wore an expensive dark blue Italian suit with a pale blue shirt, crisply pressed, which had a navy tie the exact shade as the suit. He wore plain leather highly polished soft leather shoes, his grey thick hair was collar length and gave the perfect contrast for the olive-skinned face it framed. He opened his body and invited Jake and Jonty to take a seat with a wave of the hand. They walked over the highly polished mahogany floor.

There were two club-style chairs with a charcoal grey and black stripe design with a black surround taking in the arms and legs. Opposite the chairs sat a long black sofa, a mahogany chunky coffee table sat between the two points, with two black soft leather stools completing the look. The area overlooked buildings over the New York skyline.

Jake and Jonty sat on the club chairs whilst Abano sat on the sofa opposite. A young Italian lady, Jonty guessed as mid-twenties, with a short skirt and long jet black hair almost reaching the hem of the black skirt, which, sat about six inches above the knee. She poured coffee, Gus and another guard stood beside the door to complete the picture.

"I hear from Giovanni that you were in the right place at the right time to help as he was attacked at Roberto's funeral?" Abano opened.

'*Is he quizzing me?*' Jonty thought, "Yes that's correct." he replied, not wanting to offer more information than required.

"Tell me what you need from me?" Abano asked, obviously not a man to do small talk well.

Jake explained about Em at the tree centre, that he left her for only a few minutes and the scene he found when she had disappeared. He told Abano about the phone calls Christopher received, and that they had two weeks to find and release Em.

"Why are you not using the police?" Abano enquired.

"They will not work within the timescale," Jonty said, "It's as simple as that," he added.

Abano nodded whilst tightening his lips as if to say, "I understand."

"If we help you, I must not be in a position of compromise; we may not always do things on the correct side of the law, as you would Mister Ball. We live by our rules not the rules of the government. We have no red tape, we have no judge and jury. I lead a team to protect the benefits of the team and the family."

Jake and Jonty nodded. "We understand," Jonty said.

"I am not one hundred percent sure how I can help, all I can suggest is that I put a few feelers out to see what I can do and take it from there, what do you say?"

"That sounds good enough," Jonty answered, " what do you want in return?"

"Abano smiled, "I wondered when we would get to that point." Abano's face straightened as he looked Jonty directly in the eye, he shunted forward into his seat resting his elbows on his thighs.

"Roberto is a legend in our family. As you know we are all strong catholic people. The people who disrupted the funeral of a boss is committing a sacrilege that is a crime worse than any other. The people who did this must live under a law that I cannot comprehend." He took a sip of coffee, replaced the pure white china cup.

"If we help you find the people who kidnapped your wife!" He looked at Jake, who sat statuesque opposite. Abano continued. "I want you to find the people who disrupted the funeral, murdered a friend of Roberto's and attempted to murder his brother, and a personal friend, Giovanni."

"What do you want me to do when I have found them?" Jonty asked.

"My initial view would be to kill them, but I know that will not sit comfortably with you as a police officer, so if you can get them into a Jail, I will take it from there," Abano said menacingly.

Jonty felt he was going against all he had served for and felt he was going against the pride he placed in the British justice system.

"I will do my part professionally. I don't want to know what happens after a sentence is given, should we get that far." Jonty said after a thirty-second silence.

The men shook hands, swapped mobile phone numbers "I promise to keep you updated." Abano told Jake and Jonty, he patted Jake on the shoulder as he added: "I will do all I can Jake."

CHAPTER NINE

Manchester 1938

Matthew entered Strangeways prison following a brief hearing in court where the magistrate John Swithens OBE, JP. in closing told him,

"It saddens me to see young people in front of me regularly. You are aged fifteen and have no prospects. You will be here again after your release, and you will return after that."

Matthew listened to every word, he felt a shudder go through his spine, he knew what the justice of the peace was saying was true.

Swithens continued. "Every time you return the offence will become progressively worse and more severe, where do we end up my boy, bank robbery? Murder? Where does it end? You are on this earth for a mere threescore and ten, if you are lucky. How much do you plan on it being in a cell?" Matthew was squirming with guilt, not guilt at his crime but guilt that he knew every true word, this would be a sentence for him to suffer throughout life.

' The phrase, how much do I plan on spending my life behind bars? I don't have a plan for anything! How do I get out of a cycle I have yet to begin, I don't want to live the picture he is painting!' Matthew was actively thinking. His brain was going into overdrive, He felt cold, his legs were shaking his jaw was quivering. He looked over and saw his mother crying into a handkerchief. His father never had two coins to rub together through life but was always true and honest.

Matthew could read his face as clear as the newspapers that would report his offence.

His father's face was ridden with shame, "Is this my fault, have I brought my son up to be a criminal?" Matthew wanted to reach out and tell his parents it was not their fault. It was the circumstances of the city. It was the circumstances of the day. It was the circumstances of the world for the working class.

The judge continued "There will be a bright side to some stories, unfortunately, these are very rare and only a small percentage will ever change their ways, it's not ability, it's resolve, some people will not know how to change their ways."

Swithens went quiet as he read his notes in front of him before continuing, "I am going to be lenient on you taking into consideration your age and the fact that this is your first offence. I am sentencing you to six months in Strangeways Prison. Do you have anything to say before you are taken away?"

This offer was always made, however it was rarely taken up by the convicted, sometimes obscenities cast, but never the option to speak. This was the main contribution of shock on Swithens face as Matthew said: "Yes I would like to say something."

"Thank you for the confidence and planning my future for me." He began sarcastically, then turned to look at his parents, "I will not be back here, not just to prove you wrong." he turned his head to look at the judge and continued "I have parents who are looking at this moment dejected and forlorn," His head turned to his parents again. "Father, Mother, today is a black day for our family. I do not know where my future lies but I will make this promise here and now, and may every person in this courtroom be my witness. I will not be back here after I have served the time coming to me!"

Hannah Fitzpatrick lowered her head and sobbed into a handkerchief before raising her head, pride in her eyes, and hope in her heart. She nodded to her son. That was the only acceptance Matthew needed this day.

Matthew was taken from the dock and escorted on the short Journey to Strangeways, He was lead into a large turret at the head of the building where he could see two wings coming off it at forty-five degrees. He could see there were three stories each with bars on small windows which were cells. His head filled with the fear of the unknown. He could feel his heart beating the palpitations like a sledgehammer coming from within.

He was finally escorted to a very bare reception desk, a large warden sat behind the desk. The room was large a bare floor with high ceilings, the walls were painted halfway up in moss green and cream from the halfway point to the top of the wall which met the ceiling which was also painted cream.

As he looked out of the window behind the desk he could see the tower. The tower he saw everytime he visited Manchester, it had a balcony encircling it about eighty percent up the structure, he was told this was where any hangings took place!

The prison warden sat down in his chair and welcomed Matthew with no sincerity whatsoever! Matthew didn't expect any.

"While you are here it would make sense to conform, it will make our lives easier and I promise you lad it will make your life easier too." Dave Taylor was the warden accepting Matthew today, he had lived in Salford all his life, just like Matthew he knew no different life outside crime in his early years, he fought in gang fights and looked for supremacy around the streets of Ordsall, the dock area of Salford.

A scar sat from his outer left lip and ran four inches along the length of his cheek, an obvious reminder of gang warfare, 'earning him his Salford smile.'

Taylor stood above six feet tall and had a strong muscular body under his grey uniform that only added to the drabness of the room, his jet black hair was creamed tightly to his head and shone like a piece of black silk!

He asked Matthew to strip off his clothes, threw him a block of carbolic soap and directed him to the communal showers thirty feet down the hallway. He walked the distance naked, feeling exposed, degraded, and desolate, he was escorted by two prison guards who were making fun of his undernourished body. They insisted on calling him Paddy, referring to his Irish routes that still sang through his Belfast accent.

After the shower that spewed out cold water and spluttered from a drip to a full force intermittently, he was thrown a grey inmate uniform that was three sizes too large. The material was akin to sack material and was stained where it hadn't been washed since its last owner. The shoes were of poor leather with no shoelaces. Finally, he was handed a bag, made from the same material as his uniform containing the remainder of the hard carbolic soap he had been given for his first shower, hard rough paper to be used as his toiletries and a stale crust half-round of bread.

"The bread is a delicacy as you missed lunch Paddy, welcome to Strangeways," laughed one of the guards.

He was led to a cell, as he walked all the other inmates were clattering metal plates and mugs against their cell bars and laughing at Matthew. Eventually, he was thrown into a cell about eight feet square and two beds that just fit into the room. There was another man in the room about six foot two, and two hundred pounds, he lay on the bed with one leg outstretched and hanging over the end and the other bent at the knee with his shoe on what was loosely seen as a blanket, it was ripped and torn. The man did not look at Matthew he just kept a steady stare at the damp brown stained ceiling!

   Matthew entered the room via one big push from one of the guards, he could see in the corner of the room a metal bucket filled with excrement sat in a pool of urine with a piece of the same type of paper Matthew had in his bag. The room smelt of it combined with the sweat coming from the man on the bed! Behind the man, Matthew saw a cockroach scuttle down the side of the bed at lightning speed!

   "Welcome to the savoy!" The man said after the guards had clunked the door and locked it behind them.

CHAPTER TEN

December 7th, 1997

Jonty lay back on the hotel bed, then he showered and rang Helen outlining the day's events with Abano.

"Will they help do you think?" Helen asked as she panicked over the abduction of Em.

"I don't know," Jonty replied. "They seemed all mouth and trousers." using a Manchester saying that means he talked well but is there any substance behind it? "Time will tell." he continued.

They also had a general conversation about Tommy, Helen's grandson and son of her murdered son Paul and a few other things that were going on in Helen's life at the moment but nothing deep.

Jonty lay back, he felt tired it had been a busy few days, jet lag from the flight into the USA, late last night followed by an early start this morning to meet Abano he was drifting in his mind, relaxing only the way sleep can bring.

Jonty was in that stage between awake and sleep, he thought how he had met Jake, and that Jake had stated he was Paul Jennings, Helen's son reincarnated, Jonty for obvious reasons did not believe this. Jonty travelled with Jake to London to observe a regression with a Doctor Jameson, the outcome was quite impressive with a step nearer to solving the murder of Paul Jennings, although Jonty did not appreciate the point at the time.

They were making their way to Euston Train Station to return to Manchester when something happened that brought Jonty closer to Jake in a way that can't be explained, if Darwen was still around he would have taken it back to the evolution of man in caveman days no doubt.

Jonty and Jake left Jameson's office in an increasing dark drizzle over London. They were making their way to Euston Station for the 6.00 pm train back to Manchester, as they were doing the trip in a day, no overnight stays for a copper on a police pension, which just paid enough to live comfortably and he was not yet on state pension benefits.

They were about ten minutes from Euston walking just at the back of Endsleigh Street, the streets were quiet with nobody around they both heard a northern accent mockingly say.

"Hughes and Ball ain't they a comedy act from the eighties?"

"Nah mate that was Cannon and Ball they were comedians Hughes and Ball are clowns."

They stopped and looked at each other, Jake curled a lip downwards towards Jonty. Jonty, in turn, shrugged his shoulders, they turned there were three men stood there, the smallest man was about 6-feet tall mid-fifties and carrying a baseball bat, he was of slender build and looked fit and speedy, he wore white trainers, faded jeans and white tee shirt under a denim jacket, his shoulder-length hair was wet with the rain. The second was taller by about two inches and scarred down the right side of his face, he was built of muscle and didn't carry a weapon.

'This is the guy who can handle himself,' Jonty thought, *'He doesn't need a weapon!'* He also wore a pair of boots with a good tread.

Jonty knew this would reduce slipping in a fight, he had a skin-tight tee-shirt so nobody could pull it over his head and he kept strong eye contact with Jonty, probably a mutual feeling about the fighting experience, the man weighed about two hundred and ten pounds and was no older than forty. The third man was about the same height but dressed in dark Italian style trousers and a dark grey mac with what looked like a white shirt under it, his headwear was a grey checked flat cap offering some protection from the rain.

"We don't want trouble," said the man with the cap. "Just a gentle warning, don't touch what you don't know, play with me and you play with fire, play with fire and you get burnt."

Jake and Jonty looked at each other, they had no idea at all. What was happening?

"Look," said Jake. "I think you have the wrong people, just let us go on our way and we will forget this."

Flat cap replied in a low deep aggressive voice. "We do not have the wrong people Jake."

"What is all this about?" asked Jonty.

"You know what it's about. Stay clear of digging up long-gone days."

"And if we don't?" enquired Jonty.

"I will ask my two boys to have a quiet word in your shell-like ears."

"I don't like being threatened," Jonty said.

"No threat." responded the man in the cap, "Class it as advising."

Jonty whispered to Jake through the side of his mouth. "Can you handle yourself?"

"Try me." was the response equally as quiet.

"OK," Jonty said turning back to the cap man.

"I look at it this way. I don't know what you are here for, honestly."

He turned to Jake and whispered again, "Last chance?"

"Go for it." was the reply from his wingman.

"As I was saying, the way I see it is, if we just walk away from what we don't know, you will haunt us forever, so whatever you are asking, forget it."

Flat cap nodded his face distorted and scowled. "Boys!"

The two thugs smiled that made them look like two crocodiles ready to pounce on a Zebra at the edge of a Lake. They took a step forward, the thug with the baseball bat took a double grip and strode slowly forward. Before Jonty could blink Jake was passed him, he dropped his head and shoulder almost to the floor allowing room to do a sidekick that evaded the bat to land square on his Jaw. The instant crunch told Jonty that it was a break. Jake then turned so his back was tight against the thug's chest, with the baseball bat under Jake's armpit, a sudden, quick as lightning move saw Jake's elbow land powerfully in baseball bat's nose again a crack. This time Jonty didn't hear, he was facing up to the fighter. Both boxing style toe to toe, both experienced and looking for an opening, or weakness in the profile of the other. Jonty was the first to be exposed, he felt a quick short jab in his ribs it took his breath away, but one thing he had learned was don't let it show, he then felt an uppercut to the chin.

'This guy is good and fast,' Jonty thought.

In the meantime, Jake was in the progress of pushing baseball bat's arm against its natural movement until he heard a huge yelp and the bat fell to the ground, in less than a minute baseball batman had, a broken jaw, nose and elbow joint! One final kick to the knee and baseball bat was down. Jake leaned over, picked up the bat and hurled it as far as he could throw it. He didn't want to encourage the man in the cap, although he didn't look interested after watching Jake devour his man, He looked over and could see Jonty was not getting the better of his foe in his battle, Jonty's face was bloody and he was dragging a leg.

Get to Jonty, Jake thought.

Jake hurled himself off the floor and a flying kick landed in the thug's chest, he recoiled a few yards, Jake instinctively widened his stance to give stability and in the same movement, he threw a right hook towards the thug's jaw. The thug saw it coming and raised an arm to block it, sending a counter-attack, of his own, delivering a punch straight down the centre of Jake's bodyline and landing in his mouth. Jake felt the warm liquid smelter in his mouth, he was bleeding, Jake bounced forward on his left foot delivering a perfect roundhouse kick to Thug's jaw, felt but not down. Thug seemed to grow, he growled at Jake, this man knew how to fight. Jake stood, bounced up and down keeping his body alert for any swift movement needed. Jake threw another kick hitting Thug's solar plexus, it was hard, it was low and it was perfectly struck, Thug reeled but did not go down, Jake could not believe it, nobody ever lasted this kind of pressure from him, even the American Nationals he fought in.

Thug straightened and smiled at Jake before standing side on and saying to Jake, "Is that all you have son?"

It was designed to drain Jake's confidence, and whilst it wasn't drained it was wilting. They squared with each other.

Flat cap shouted, "Jack behind you!"

To late Jonty dropped the baseball bat over thug's head like a woodsman felling a tree, the thug fell to the ground, first to his knees, and just to help him on his way, Jake gave another roundhouse kick at the same time Jonty delivered another baseball bat strike across the back of the neck,

They turned to the man in the cap, "What is this about?" Jonty screamed.

The Man turned and ran with pace, Jake and Jonty did not have the energy to chase after their tussle. They both walked towards the station until they were out of sight out of sight of their two opponents, simultaneously bent down with their hands on their knees and took deep breaths, Jonty put his arm around Jake puffing and panting.

"I have three things to say, one are you sure you can handle yourself?" he laughed then straightened up, "and two, I don't know who they are or what it's about, but a cage has been rattled," he took a breath still breathing heavily and told Jake, "I'm in."

Jake spoke, "You said you had three points what's the third?"

Jonty's response was quick. "Next time you throw a bloody baseball bat away, don't throw it as far!!" they both laughed. Jonty saw Jake with fresh eyes.

Thug turned out to be Jack Evans. He worked for Roberto and Giovanni. He met up a few months later, with Jonty and gave an insight on how Roberto's family operated. This information led to the prosecution of James "Shep" Shepherd, the former friend and colleague of Jonty's, and the involvement of Superintendent John Quinn, who at this moment in time was on the run somewhere in the world, but at this point, he had disappeared off the face of it with no tracks or leads to go off.

'I must get back in touch with Evan's when I get home, I can't help but think Quinn is involved here somehow!' Jonty thought before the power of sleep took over!

CHAPTER ELEVEN.

MANCHESTER 1938

"My name is Danny Turner!" the man said to Matthew, "What are you in for? You're a little young to be in here aren't you?"

"Matthew Fitzpatrick, I am in here for actual bodily harm."

Turner laughed, "What on a sparrow? What harm could you do to anybody?"

Matthew ran at the man with rage in his eyes, his fists were swinging like windmills, the small room meant that he reached Turner in less than a second. Turner was still laughing as he bear-hugged Matthew, turned him around and squeezed him tightly around his torso.

"My we are feisty aren't we," Turner said through laughing teeth.

Matthew was still swinging and kicking but it was only fresh air on the receiving end, Turner threw him on the bed.

"No offence meant." Turner laughed and stretched out a hand to make a handshake, Matthew met the hand.

"That will do you no good in here Matthew, there are men who wait for such things, it's a sport to them, it passes the time, keep your head low, do you hear me?"

Matthew nodded.

"Well let's pretend that never happened," Turner said with a large grin that made Matthew feel he could do nothing but return it.

The first week passed for Matthew as prescribed, as expected, monotonous, as expected, and boring as expected. One thing he didn't bank on was how quickly he would get friendly with Turner.

Turner was sentenced for five years in his part in planning a bank robbery that turned out drastically wrong, it was meant to be a straightforward job, Jason Smith was to go up to the counter, hand a note to the teller, the gun was only there to add fear and panic into people!

All was going to plan. Jason approached the cashier. Davey Smith, Jason's brother, entered the door and closed it behind them, leaving only a handful of customers and staff in the banking hall. The cashier was loading the bag with cash when a customer in the banking hall, a would-be hero rugby tackled Jason to the ground another man went to help him, Davey shot the rifle, it hit the first man in the leg he grimaced with pain. The second man turned and stopped.

"Ok he said I have stopped now!" he said as he backed away from Jason.

Davey didn't know what to do, he panicked, he was only seventeen, he didn't want to kill anybody. He instinctively pulled the trigger and the man fell over to a motionless position.

"Get up!" Davey shouted, the man never moved, "Get up!" he shouted again, still no movement. Davey began crying, he went cold, a slow-motion era took place all around him, a silence and brief serenity, He could not hear the pandemonium he caused. Women were screaming, men were trying to help the two injured men. Davey felt like he was underwater watching fish swim by in the barrier reef, all quiet and serene, then Jason pushed him.

"Move! Let's get out of here now!"

Suddenly all the noise came back to Davey as his senses returned. They rushed out of the bank to the getaway car where Turner was waiting. Just as the car doors slammed a police car stopped in front of them and another behind. They were caught red-handed.

That was three years ago and Turner delivered exemplary behavior, as he wanted to be out at the first possible opportunity!

After two week's Turner told Matthew there was somebody he wanted him to meet. They sat waiting for the person to enter their twenty-three-hour confined cell.

"You must be Matthew said the voice that was behind the man dressed as the regular parish priest, stood in front of them in a black cassock. Father O'Gorman returned from delivering mass to the prisoners sentenced to be hung, he delivered mass every week. The congregation numbers were always strong. "It's funny how all men turn to God in an hour of need." He once said to Turner.

Mathew, a Catholic by religion, was not a strong practitioner, although his parents were still strong to the faith. This made Matthew respect the man in front of them.

"Father O'Gorman visits me every week after mass for the sentenced men, I take confession and communion," Turner said in a friendly manner

"I am supposed to ease some of their pain, I don't think I succeed. I will say though, I don't believe when we execute a person that it's the same person who committed the crime. I do believe people can change." Father O'Gorman said. "That is why I will work until my dying breath to help all the people I can in here and anywhere," he added.

Both Matthew and Turner took confession, although privacy was not a privilege allowed, followed by communion.

This became a regular occurrence for Matthew. Having an inquisitive mind he would ask Father O'Gorman all types of questions regarding the bible, what was initially a ten-minute visit had quickly gathered in time and the priest would be in the cell with Matthew and Turner for an hour at a time.

Matthew was bright despite his hard upbringing with little education, he felt that discussions with Father John were invigorating and he looked forward to them so much. He and Turner would debate the bible. Matthew would not be afraid of challenging the bible or the scriptures, one day he was putting a case over from the gospel of St Luke.

"Answer me this Father John?" Matthew said. "The last time Joseph is mentioned in the Bible is when Jesus was twelve years old. Returning from a trip to Jerusalem, Jesus separated from His parents, who eventually found Him in the temple conversing with the teachers. Ironically, it was at that time Jesus announced he had to be about his heavenly father's business,"

Father John smiled at Matthew and answered "The theory that Joseph had died by the time Jesus was an adult is given further credibility by the fact that, when Jesus was on the cross, he made arrangements for his mother to be cared for by the apostle John. Joseph must have been dead by the time of the crucifixion, or Jesus would never have committed Mary to John. If Joseph were still alive, Jesus would not say, "Now, Mother, I'm going to commit you to John." Joseph would have rightly responded, "Wait a minute; it is my responsibility to take care of her." Only a widow could have rightly be given into the care of someone outside the immediate family.

It is thought by many that Joseph died sometime after Jesus began His public ministry. This is unlikely, because, if Joseph had died during the three-year ministry of Christ, that would have been a major event; Jesus undoubtedly would have gone to the funeral with His disciples, and at least one of the Gospel writers would have recorded it. Although we do not know for sure, the most likely scenario is that Joseph died sometime before Jesus began His earthly ministry.

This would be a normal discussion, sometimes Matthew putting Father John into corners he struggled to get out of and sometimes answering questions to the full.

One thing was certain, the more Matthew questioned Catholicism more questions raised. His faith was being restored. If his parents had laid the foundations Father John was building the house of faith brick by brick.

Matthew's term reached an end, there had been hard at times, the men in the main were never hard on him due to his tender years and thin weak body, There was no threat of him being the top dog, so everything just meandered along.

As he prepared to leave he shook hands with Turner, they helped to keep each other sane, how well do you have to know somebody when you share a bucket for a toilet? Using it in the presence of each other daily. You sweat together on hot summer days, you shiver together on cold winter days and you kill rats, mice, cockroaches, and other vermin just to keep the standard of your accommodation as clean as you can.

They agreed to meet up again on Turner's release in nine months time.

Father John was waiting outside to give Matthew a ride back to Ancoats where an eager family were waiting to throw a surprise welcome home party.

CHAPTER TWELVE

December 8th, 1997

"Jonty Wake up!" Jonty jolted into the world of the living with a loud banging on his hotel door, it was Jake.

"Jake, what do you want at this unearthly hour?"

Jonty it's ten in the morning Abano has been trying to contact you, he messaged me instead. He has one of his men picking us up in half an hour!" Jonty looked at the screen on his mobile phone it read 'eight missed calls!' *'I must stop putting it on silent mode,'* he thought.

Jonty was still groggy and not quite sure where he was, it then became clear where he was and why he was there. "OK, I will meet you downstairs at ten-thirty he shouted through."

He quickly showered and shaved, threw on a pair of navy chinos he packed along with a cream coloured Henri Lloyd crew neck tee-shirt, which didn't quite look right on a mid-sixties man with a paunch. The look completed with a pair of mid tan loafers bragging two tassels sitting proudly on top of each foot.

He walked out of the elevator at ten twenty-eight, Jake looked at his watch and smiled "Bang on time old man!" He said in his mid-west accent.

"I Beg your pardon, two minutes early actually," Jonty replied with a smile.

Jake also dressed casually, he had a pair of Levi 501's on with a red Hugo Boss collared tee shirt and red Adidas training shoes, his blonde hair had grown from short to wavy collar length over the period Jonty had known him. He was physically fit and young. At twenty-six, he also possessed a black belt in karate and fought for the national team, an asset Jonty was pleased to find out when they had the grapple at Euston Station the year earlier.

At ten-thirty prompt Gus walked through the door, people stopped and stared at the man-mountain as he walked into the foyer. He had never quite got used to this reaction from people wherever he went.

He smiled and walked up to Jonty and Jake, even Jonty looked small in the presence of Gus! As usual, Gus was smartly dressed in a light grey suit, highly polished black shoes, finished off with a grey shirt and tie.

Gus was in a different car today, he opened the door of the navy BMW X5 to greet Jonty and Jake with a cream leather interior, they both climbed into the back as Gus closed the door and assumed his normal position of sitting in the front next to the chauffeur!

The BMW snaked its way from the hotel and into St Colombus Circle. It exited the roundabout towards Sixty-Fifth Street and then a right onto central park west drive, after about half a mile the car turned up a large tree drive with a large house sat at the end, a round manicured lawn was circulated by a driveway that allowed several cars to stop at the main entrance of the house. As Gus opened the door for the two passengers they both looked in awe at the fabulous views taking in central park.

They strode to the twelve-foot high double doors, which, painted navy blue almost matched the colour of the BMW parked on the drive.

They went through the large front door. Abano walked from a door with a welcoming smile on his face and a hand ready to shake. There was a large entrance hall to welcome them, the hall boasted, pearl white tiling, the hallway was large with four doors running into pentagon-shaped walls, in the middle was a staircase that was around ten feet wide, there were two spindled handrails made of what looked like old mahogany going up the full length of the stairs.

  Abano turned to Jonty and Jake. "You must be thirsty, coffee? Something a little stronger maybe?"

  "Coffee white with one will be fine thanks." Jonty said, Jake nodded in agreement, "Coffee for me too please Mister Abano."

  "Hey what's this Mr. Abano? Gino, please, coffee it is."

  "Make yourself comfortable I will organise your drink."

  They were invited into a room with a window on each side wall which one held a view over a small lake with a red and white rowing boat on it, Some maintenance to the boat was needed as it looked in need of some paint, the oars sat either side as the boat sat just on the land bank. The other window took in a forest of trees with a wood shavings path leading up through the trees. Jonty looked around the room, the house was contemporary, he preferred period but there was no mistaking this was bursting its banks with class and expense. He sat down on one of the two cream modern leather sofa's facing each other. Jake sat beside him. There was a mahogany coffee table running in-between the sofa's, although there was nothing on the table and its nakedness added to the class of the room. Jonty looked to his left and a modern white bookcase stretched along the wall, ceiling to floor, there were probably two thousand books in the bookcase with a sliding ladder at one end that could be used to get the higher books that utilised every inch of the fifteen-foot ceiling. To his right was an inglenook fireplace made in the same cream as the tiles in the hallway and a log burning stove that was about four feet wide, there were another four feet either side of the fire with seats in the inglenook to keep you warm in the winter. The room smelt of nothing but the flowers that sat in large light grey vases sending out the fresh blossom smell of summer flowers, there was a vase in each corner and all sat on matching grey marble and oak jardinières.

"Thank you for coming at short notice." Abano said, "I will get straight to the point, I think we have some information about Emily's situation."

"Do you know where she is?" Jake asked with great enthusiasm.

"No, we don't know where she is….Yet."

"Well, what do you know?" Jake asked a little flatter this time.

"We have had many people looking for any information that may be out there." Abano broke off for a second.

"Luca the TV please," he shouted through to an adjacent room.

A wiry man walked through in a shiny silver suit, it looked more fitting for a disco than a working suit, it was not of the same cut as Abano's or Gus's. He walked to the TV and picked up a remote control that fired up the seventy-inch screen in the corner of the room.

A not to clear picture started showing on the screen as the man on the TV in the white shirt and brown slacks strolled across what looked like a concrete wall at the side of a dock!

"This is Paulo Ramirez an Argentine who works for a drug baron. Information tells us Billy Jones owes him money, a lot of money. the Sartori godfather owes Ramirez two million dollars for a supply of cocaine to the UK. This has not been paid.

Jonty interrupted, "That will be because I managed to get Jones' assets froze in the bank account he was laundering money through."

Abano continued, "That makes sense, anyway word on the street now is that Jones is holding Emily hostage to blackmail her Father to pay the debt, He would not want to cross the drug barons."

Jonty replied, "That's great work but are you any nearer to locating Emily?"

"Yes and no." Abano answered, Jonty and Jake looked at him quizzically.

"We don't know where she is but we do know where a Sartori family captain is, and because he is in town, we assume he is managing the kidnap."

"Who is the captain?" Jake asked.

Abano replied, "One, we are not familiar with a man in the name of Ken Fitzroy, Have you heard of him?" He looked at Jonty.

Jonty nodded, "unfortunately only too well." He replied.

Jonty gained most of his information from the family informer Jack Evans, Evans wanted no payment for information, his only goal was to leave the family without threat or harm to him and his family. He needed Jonty to make arrests for this to become a reality.

Evans told Jonty that Fitzroy was a hard man who was his boss, his caporegime, or captain in the mafia terminology.

Evans outlined the family structure to Jonty in a meeting they held in Chester. "The next level is the caporegime. This would be Ken Fitzroy. The capo is the captain or lieutenant of a division within the mafia. He heads a large crew of soldiers, like Steve Pitt and myself. He can order them to do anything, such as murder, assault, bombing… anything. The captain reports directly to a boss or underboss, who hands down the instructions. He ranks much higher in the hierarchy of the mafia. He is also in charge of handling most of the money."

He passed this information to Abano, who just nodded with no reaction showing on his sun-tanned wrinkled face.

Abano was dressed in a smart casual burgundy jacket over a sky blue shirt, identical in shade were matching trousers finished off with a pair of burgundy loafers. His sunglasses sat on his forehead with the Gucci mark emblazoned on the arms.

"What is the next step?" Jonty asked.
"It will take a few days to close in on Mr. Fitzroy then we will let you know?"

Be Careful Fitzroy is a very dangerous man." Jonty advised.
"Thank you." Abano, replied in a non-concerned way "I will be in touch."
With that, the meeting ended.

CHAPTER THIRTEEN.

MANCHESTER 1941

Matthew had a different view on life following his prison sentence. His faith in Catholicism had been reinvigorated, as promised he met up with Turner who held similar views. Their friendship continued beyond the release of the prison walls.

On the day of Danny Turner's release Matthew was there to meet him, he had walked the two miles from his home to the prison gate, the gate opened and out walked Danny with a big grin on his face, the two men embraced each other for a good ten seconds, on releasing the hug Danny said.

"Look at you, you are no longer the underweight underfed boy who walked into our cell and wanted to fight the world."

Matthew smiled and replied, "I am spending a lot of time with Father O'Gorman. I am seriously thinking of becoming a priest."

"Well done you." was Danny's reply, genuinely feeling pleased for Matthew.

Danny was correct about Matthew filling out, he had grown from the nine stone seven-pound boy he met on entering the cell to a fourteen stone mass of muscle. He regularly frequented the boxing club and had built up a solid reputation for his fighting skills, not losing a bout in the Manchester district in fourteen fights.

The two could not be dressed differently on the hot mid-June afternoon, the heat was just reaching its maximum,

Matthew was dressed for the weather, wearing a white short-sleeved crew neck tee shirt with a pair of light blue jeans and a pair of American style black and white baseball boots. Danny wore the same old grey suit he entered prison in, which was now at least two sizes too large after living on meager prison slops, they called food. He wore a white shirt that was also big and had faded into grey, His black leather shoes greyed at the toe due to seeing no polish in his prison term.

"I hope you have nothing on this afternoon Father O'Gorman would love to see you," Matthew told his friend.

"No the Queen has cancelled my knighthood for today" Danny replied with a smile.

Danny and Matthew walked to the entrance gates at the church. The walls and pathway leading up to the door were cobbled and pristine. St Theresa's was renowned in the dioceses for the best kept church, and people always questioned where the funding came from.

They walked down the path with graves neatly sat on either side, Danny briefly stopped at one and made the sign of the cross, Matthew watched him, the stone read.

Here Lies Jonathon Turner
Died 18 May 1907 aged 46
Also lies his beloved wife Margaret
Died 1921 aged 61

"My great grandparents," Danny said.

As they reached the door, it opened before they could knock.

Mrs. Milthorpe, affectionately known as Mrs. Mop was waiting for the men to arrive. She had been Father O'Gorman's housekeeper for ten years now and was the only person who could tell the aging priest anything she liked, and got away with it.

"Come in, Come in, She said with a lot of enthusiasm. "Danny, I haven't seen you since you were, what, nine, ten maybe?"

"It must be about that long Mrs. Milthorpe." Danny Answered.

"And how are your Mother and Father?" She quizzed.

"They are well. I am going to see them after seeing Father O'Gorman."

"I shall have a word with him, who does he think he is having priority over your parents," Mrs.Milthorpe said.

"Sit down I will make you both a nice hot cup of tea, then she looked out of the window at the burning sun. "Or would you prefer some cool lemonade?"

"I will tell Father you are here." She said, before scurrying off out of the vestibule they had been ushered into. Her short wide frame waddled out of the door, she wore a light blue denim style dress covered by a white apron, her thick grey curly hair tied in a bun at the back, her, feet donned a pair of pink slippers with dark brown thick stockings tucked in them.

The room was twelve feet square, the walls were dark oak making it a gloomy room, it smelt musty with visible particles of dust floating by where the narrow arched windows let the sunlight through.

They sat in matching chairs, which were an antique green chesterfield shape, where the arms were the same height at the back. Directly in front of them was a large desk matching the colour of the oak walls with a green leather centrepiece matching the colour of the chairs, on the other side of the desk sat an empty captain style chair, again in the same green leather but this chair had wooden spindles between the backrest and the seat. Behind the seat was a white marble statue of Christ on the cross.

"Pure Italian marble, the best in the world," said a familiar voice. they had not noticed Father O'Gorman enter the room. They were both transfixed by the statue.

"Nothing is done on the cheap here is it father," Danny said.

"No Danny we at St Theresa's have a very good benefactor who asks for a little favour now and again," he said with a wry smile. "Which is a good starting point regarding the things I would like to discuss today."

Danny and Matthew looked at the priest as Mrs. Mop brought in the cold lemonade, "Just what the doctor ordered." Said the priest with a smile on his face.

Danny told the Priest and Matthew about the latest prison gossip and how grateful he was for the two of them getting him through it, another fifteen minutes of idle gossip continued.

Father O'Gorman changed the direction of the discussion. "I am not of good health these days and my wish, after I have gone is to keep this church pristine as it is now."

"Father you're not going anywhere," Matthew interrupted.

"Matthew I wish you were correct but I am an old man now and I need people I can trust to continue my work. The beneficiary I speak of is a man called Roberto Sartori. I have passed your names on to him, he will contact you in the future. You must help with whatever he asks, Promise me?"

Both Danny and Matthew had that much faith in the priest they promised without hesitation.

"Now Danny I have kept you too long from your parents, you must go and see them, they will be anxious to see you."

CHAPTER FOURTEEN

December 9th, 1997

It was 9.00 am when the room telephone rang, Jonty picked the receiver up.

"Jonty, Gus will be waiting in the car at nine-thirty outside the hotel's main entrance, be on time." Jonty put the phone down

"They are getting very chatty that lasted all of ten seconds, any news?"

We have to be outside the hotel in thirty minutes, Gus will be waiting," Jonty replied, "I don't know any more than that."

At nine-thirty prompt, the black limousine arrived, a new driver now in place, not the normal chauffer, there was a black Mercedes E class behind it with four men sat in it.

Jonty looked at Jake, "This isn't to take us on the beach for the day." He said.

They climbed in the rear seats of the Cadillac XTS Limousine, the grey leather smelt like it was no older than a week, the windows were blacked out, two cups of coffee sat in front of Jonty and Jake. Gus turned around and spoke through a speaker in the curtesy screen which separated them.

"We know where one, Mr. Kenneth Fitzroy is, he is in Boone, we have a private jet leaving from Newark to Des-Moines at eleven. We will tell you more on the plane." Gus turned off the speaker and the rest of the journey was in silence.

Jonty and Jake had agreed not to talk in the car because they could be overheard and could say something they may regret. They just looked at each other now and again anxiously.

The car arrived at the airport and approached a different building than the one they landed at, there were no queues to join as there were at the check-in booths. This time the car just drove under a tunnel onto the runway towards a jet sat waiting with the engines running.

The jet was an Embraer Legacy 600 Model. It was an impressive jet. The car stopped, Gus and the driver got out of the car, and the man who Jake and Jonty new as the normal chauffeur walked towards the car ready to drive it back.

The four men behind climbed out of the Mercedes Jonty looked and thought *'This looks more like a Rugby Union front line.'*

All four men were built strong, all over six foot four; the only thing that could make them look small was Gus. Gus made sure everybody was clear of the cars as he waved them to the steps leading into the Embraer. Jonty entered the Jet only to be amazed by its luxury, there were thirteen seats, which were required for the eight of them given the size of these men.

All of Abano's men wore black suits with pristine white shirts and black ties, polished shoes, and sunglasses. Gus saw Jonty looking at them and said: "We always dress appropriately for a funeral."

As the plane took off a waitress served brunch, which was welcome to both Jonty and Jake as they had no time for breakfast following the phone call. They enjoyed eggs benedict with fresh juice, followed by watermelon and hot fresh coffee. Gus laughed at Jonty as he poured milk in his drink, "You will be Italian by the end of the day."

Halfway through the four-hour flight, Gus asked Jonty and Jake if he could have a word,

They all made their way to the rear of the aircraft.

When settled Gus began to speak, "Roberto Sartori was a very good friend of mine, I have known him since I was in short trousers. I hear what happened at his funeral was disgusting, not the mafia way. We may have enemies, all of us, but we always show respect to families. That is what sets us apart from criminals. We just run a respectful business. People may get hurt sometimes but we are just business people. There was no respect shown here, we will avenge the misdoings, and give Giovanni the maximum respect he deserves from Roberto's funeral." He went quiet for a second. "If this was his grandson's doing there will be no forgiveness."

Jonty and Jake stayed quiet but were having similar thoughts about *'just a business?'*

"You both agreed with Giovanni that if we do it our way, find and release Emily from her captors then no more is said. Agreed?" He looked at Jonty knowing he was a UK detective.

Jake and Jonty looked at each other and said unanimously. "Agreed!"

The plane landed four hours and fifteen minutes after take-off. They were met by two five series BMWs with drivers in full chauffeur uniforms who doffed their caps acknowledging all the customers one by one.

They drove across from the airport and to the Newark Liberty International airport hotel, where they had a conference room pre-booked. Waiting for them there was Paulo Conchetti. Conchetti was a captain of the Mainiero family, who operated around Ohio and would always want to know what was happening in the area. Alfredo Mainiero, the family godfather had been involved with several operations alongside the Abano family. Gus and Paulo looked good friends they hugged and laughed in Italian to each other, no doubt many a story to tell.

There were now eight men all walking to the conference room that had been pre-booked. The room was spacious enough for business conferences to hold around thirty people. It was modern and comfortable, with projectors if needed for PowerPoint presentations or just flip charts for the non-tech people. Gus used neither, he was not going to leave a trail.

All the men sat down and discussed the situation. Gus introduced Paulo and the five men Jonty and Jake did not know, they were unable to recall their names five minutes later but gave a courteous nod as Gus introduced them.

Gus began to speak. "We owe Paulo and his team a lot for getting the investigation to this stage and the Mainiero family, as always, have been of great assistance to the Abano family. Thank you, Paulo." Both men nodded at each other, Paulo gave a general nod around the room.

Gus continued, "Paulo would you like to update us on the Emily abduction?"

Paulo took over, "Thank you, Gus, we have learned that a Ken Fitzroy, who is part of the UK Sartori family has overseen the abduction." The room had his full attention and was quiet, he continued. "There was a closing of UK Bank accounts held by the Sartori's which has left them in debt to many people." Paulo let his words sink in, before continuing, "This leaves some of the top people in the family, including Billy Jones, the current godfather, with their lives at risk." All went silent.

Paulo continued, "We believe that the group is now a splinter group from the Sartori family and thus have disrespected the Cosa Nostra. We therefore no longer recognise them as a family. Our allegiance is with Giovanni Sartori, not Billy Jones." Gus was nodding in approval as Paulo finished this part of his talk with "Therefore anything that happens to any member of the splinter group will receive no repercussions from the Mainiero family," He looked at Gus.

Gus spoke, "I can confirm that both Don Abano and Don Mainiero have discussed this and the Abano family is in full support of not recognising Billy Jones and the splinter group of the Sartori family. Also, I can confirm that it has been agreed that Giovanni Sartori is now Don Giovanni, in the eyes of our families and all the New York families including the Rossi family, the family closest to the Sartori family."

Gus looked Jonty square in the eyes "Therefore any actions taken against the criminal Billy Jones and his mob is fair game in our eyes."

"Paulo will outline our plan to return Emily safe and sound back to her family."

CHAPTER FIFTEEN

Manchester February 1945.

Matthew Fitzpatrick qualified as a priest in nineteen-forty five, following six years of training under the masterful guidance of Father O'Gorman. He completed a one-year introductory programme known as the *Propaedeutic Year*, where he worked closely with, Bishop Condron, who found Matthew both enlightening and intelligent and quickly recommended him for progress onto the Formation Course, then finally The Seminary *Course of Formation* course which involved placements in parishes of the diocese in which Matthew gained practical, pastoral and liturgical skills.

He was now the parish priest of St Theresa's and here he stood on a cold February day with the snow falling heavily around in a pitch-black heavily-laden sky watching the coffin of Father O'Gorman being laid to rest. He read a vocation prayer for his mentor, friend, and from a life of crime, his saviour.

Take, Lord, and Receive

Take, Lord, and receive all my liberty, my memory,
My understanding and my entire will.
All I have and call my own.
Whatever I have or hold you have given me.
I return it all to you and surrender it wholly
To be governed by your will.

Give me only your love and your grace
Until I am rich enough and ask for nothing more.
Amen.

There were hundreds of people at the funeral, the parishioners loved the man who respected each one of them and always took pride in having the wealthiest church fund in the north-west of England.

One of the people in the congregation that day was Roberto Sartori and his wife Antonia. He walked over to Matthew and introduced himself. Matthew knew the name from Father O'Gorman and knew of his large contributions to the church. He also remembered the comment Father O'Gorman made about completing a few favours for Mister Sartori.

"Good morning Father I am Roberto Sartori, Father O'Gorman may have mentioned me in passing. What an awful day to lay to rest a fantastic Father to our parish."

"Good morning Mr. Satori."

Roberto interrupted, "Father, Roberto please, and this is my wife Antonia, known as Toni"

"Pleased to meet you both, Father O'Gorman told me you are a major beneficiary for our causes, thank you."

"No problem Father, and there is much more to come in the future I am sure. The church is an opportunity for the working-class people of the parish to feel welcome and protected; I want to support them through the church as much as I can."

Roberto looked Matthew in the eye, "If you need anything Father please do not hesitate to ask, unfortunately, my brother Giovanni could not make today, but I am sure you will meet, in the meantime thank you for a lovely service, I must let you get out of this dreadful weather."

Father Matthew Fitzpatrick had finally met the renowned Roberto Sartori.

CHAPTER SIXTEEN.

December 9th, 1997

Paulo thanked Gus for his support and continued. "Our intelligence tells us that there is a working cell from the UK active in Boone." He looked around the room and saw every eye glued to his speech, Paulo liked power, he liked to control, he liked people listening to his every word.

"We are told it is headed up by Ken Fitzroy, Pat O'Neill, and Steve Pitt." Jonty knew all of these names, he thought of the story Evans told him, about how Billy had recruited them.

Fitzroy was a no-nonsense hoodlum from Liverpool. Fitzroy and his close friend, Pat O'Neill, had been up in and around the dock area of Liverpool. They ran a small, illegal import and export business trafficking drugs to and from Liverpool docks. They then sold the drugs on the streets of the city.

When Billy heard about their tough reputation, he drove to Walton Vale, a tough area of Liverpool, and offered them a job working for him on their turf. They initially refused, Fitzroy told Billy he could work for them if he knew what was good for him.

Billy smiled and waved his arm in a forwarding motion to the driver of the hired E class Mercedes. The two scallies laughed.

"So, you're looking for a ruck?" Fitzroy said.

"No," Billy replied. "I want to work with you, not against you."

Fitzroy sneered at Billy. He was six foot four and spent a lot of time working out; his arms looked like they were going to burst under the tight short sleeves of the Nike T-shirt.

"I don't like Mancs," he said, using the term used for somebody from Manchester.

Fitzroy continued. "Don't come on our turf and tell us how to do business." He was now glaring at Billy. "It's either my way, or I am going to knock you back to Moses."

The two men advanced towards Billy, the driver eased out of the car door and was walking to join the 'discussion'. Fitzroy glanced towards the car, he looked again, Steve Pitt, Fitzroy recognising him.

"Steve, how are you?" Pitt remained straight-faced and put his hand in the pocket of his expensive-looking, calf-length black leather coat. Fitzroy knew that Steve Pitt probably had a gun in the pocket. He also knew that he would take anybody on head to head in the city, except Steve Pitt.

"Well, you never said you were a friend of Steve's," said Fitzroy with a noticeable change in demeanour. "That makes things different."

Billy looked at Fitzroy. "In what way is it different?"

Fitzroy laughed. "In a way that we can discuss things."

Twenty years had passed since that meeting and it did not take a mathematician to work out that there was more money for Fitzroy and O'Neill working for Billy than they would ever earn working alone. Fitzroy had been loyal ever since.

Now here they were in Des-Moines, Ohio with his best friend's wife abducted, and held for ransom. Jonty thought of how tough Fitzroy was, not only was Fitzroy here he had Pat O'Neill and Steve Pitt with him. Jonty's heart sank. *These family boys think they are good, but they are dealing with the best Billy has.* Jonty thought.

Paulo continued. "Our intelligence tells us the three of them are going to eat at a top restaurant tonight. We believe it is the appropriately named L'ultima Cena!" everybody laughed except Jonty and Jake Gus interrupted, whilst still laughing, "In English it means The last supper."

Jonty smiled thinking, *these people think this a cakewalk, they don't understand how dangerous these three are.*

Paulo continued, "We plan to let them get comfortably into the meal, then Luigi, Alessandro, and Piero will go in the front door, We have arranged for two to enter from the rear door, Nani and Luca that will be you. We have arranged for one of our trusted employees Aria to let you in. Santi you will be at a table near the three of them eating as a couple, the meal is on me, although I doubt you will finish it." The room all laughed again, and again with the exception of Jonty and Jake.

"The important thing is we take them alive or we will never find out where Emily is." Paulo added.

"We managed to get hold of a local anaesthetic from a doctor on our payroll, it will put them to sleep. This is where the risk lies. We need to administer it with a needle before we do they will be alerted and fighting, they may, even have guns! The person who will administer it is Gus, for obvious reasons." They all looked at the man-mountain.

"The cars will pick us up from here at seven-thirty, In the meantime, we must all be hungry, they do fantastic Italian food here, let's eat."

CHAPTER SEVENTEEN.

New York 1921

Benito Rossi and Roberto Sartori Senior, Roberto's father, had been friends from childhood in the late nineteenth century when there was no money in poverty-stricken Sicily. They grew up together and, rather than work the vineyards or land for a pittance, they decided to take their future income in their own hands. They earned their living running a very basic form of protection racket, although the proceeds were never enough to allow a comfortable living, it was always a day to day hand to mouth activity.

In 1908 Roberto Senior and Benni decided to emigrate, as many Sicilians did at that time to start a new life and dreams outside Sicily and the poverty it brought. Benni chose New York whilst Roberto Senior chose Liverpool, England. Their paths could not have been more different, Roberto carried on with basic crimes, extortion, and robbery leading a poverty-ridden life, whilst Benni chose the life of a family don in an ever-growing Italian crime family culture.

Roberto senior died of tuberculosis contributed by the low standard of living he encountered in England.

On hearing of the death, Benni invited Roberto Junior to New York, Roberto accepted the invitation, travelling to New York on the liner *Mauretania*. Roberto arranged to meet Benni at Ellis Island in an attempt to strike an agreement on the export of alcohol, in the current prohibition era, they were to discuss top quality Scottish and Irish whiskey for a New York City that could drink all it could consume and more!

"Roberto, you look well. My, you have grown." Benni said.

Roberto was eight-years-old when he and his family left Sicily for Liverpool in 1908. He was now a young 21-year-old man. He wore his best brown tweed suit, which was the only suit he owned, a flat cap, and a pair of boots that came halfway up his calves. His jet-black hair reached down to his collar, he carried the Sartori good looks. He was six feet tall and full of energy with a background of fighting on the streets of Liverpool, earning a life full of petty crime and competing with the Irish. Overall, he made ends meet. He lived with his parents and brother, Giovanni, in a one-bedroom house that was damp encouraging cockroaches and rats by the dozen. It was no wonder his father contracted and later died from TB.

Benni, on the other hand, appeared to have found a wealth that Roberto could only dream of, Benni wore a pure white shirt that sat neatly beneath an expensive-looking Milan-made navy pinstripe suit on the day they met. Roberto noticed the hand stitching on the lapel. Benni looked healthy, with a smart haircut. His hair had turned salt and pepper and, with his Sicilian olive skin, it made him look a picture of health.

"Mr. Rossi, it is so good to see you again," said Roberto. "My mother sends her love."

Benni smiled. "Hey, what's all this Mr. Rossi? You are a handsome young man now, and it's Benni."

Both men smiled. Benni put both his hands on Roberto's arms and stood square on facing him. "I was sorry to hear about your father, we were like brothers. I want to help you and your family for old time's sake, febene?"

"Thank you, Mr... erm... Benni."

"Hey, what am I thinking," Benni said. "You have travelled, you must be hungry. Let's go eat." He turned around, to a man sitting on a wall at the side of the road. "Paulo, get the car, we are going to take our guest to the restaurant Piccolo Italia."

Roberto had not noticed the man due to his concentration on meeting Benni again.

"I need to go through immigration first," Roberto mentioned to Benni, indicating to the immigration signs where he had to have his passport stamped.

"Nonsense, come with me." Benni took Roberto by the arm and walked past the queue of people to the immigration guard. "Hey, Charlie, this is my friend, we are okay to go through, no?"

"Go straight through, Mr. Rossi, and have a nice day."

"Thank you, Charlie," Benni replied.

With that, Roberto walked into America.

Roberto had been in New York for three months when, one evening, whilst dining at Piccolo Italia with Benni and a few close confidantes, his head turned to see an elegantly dressed woman. She was tall and wore an olive green pair of loose-fitting trousers perfectly cut in length, skimming a pair of low-heeled court shoes. A blouse of a paler green neatly tucked into the trousers with a cream belt separating the blouse and trousers. Draped around her perfectly formed shoulders she wore a cream, finely knitted cardigan. She was talking to a man, who was also smartly dressed in a black suit. He had short, neatly cut hair. The man's back faced Roberto, but he could see over his shoulder the perfectly formed face of the woman, her features shrouded by jet-black hair that hung in luxurious waves down past her neck, terminating just above the point where her shoulder blades began.

 The girl's beauty stopped Roberto in his tracks. She looked over her companion's shoulder towards Roberto. It was the shortest of glances before she looked away again within a second. She continued talking to the man. After about a minute, the man ordered what appeared to be two more coffees for the girl and himself, allowing the girl a little break to again look at Roberto. She smiled. Roberto's mouth went dry as he smiled back.

 She turned back to her companion and started talking to him again. As he ended his quick conversation with the bartender, the girl gave one final look towards Roberto and smiled again. The couple stood up from the high stools at the bar and walked out. The man was settling the bill and not re-ordering; however, there was enough time for the girl to look over her shoulder and give one last smile towards Roberto as she left the building. Roberto left with a dry throat and a yearning to see this woman again.

 A few days after Roberto's first sighting of the girl in green, fate took over. He saw her walking past Times Square with a friend; this time, though, it was a girlfriend and not a male. He stopped and smiled. She smiled back.

 "Hello," he said. "Long time no see!"

 She smiled, then, turned to her friend. "Jancy, I will call you later, to arrange lunch," Janey gave a knowing smile and left.

 "I was thinking of an espresso, would you care to join me?" asked Roberto.

 "I prefer an Americano, it takes longer to drink." answered the coy beauty.

"Will your boyfriend wonder where you are?" quizzed Roberto, hitting the awkward question square in the face.

"Boyfriend?" asked the girl. "Ah, you mean Alfi, my brother! He was in the Piccolo Italia for some family business. We have a fish distribution company and Alfi has been trying to get into Piccolo, without much success."

She looked at him. "What do you do?"

"I am in the retail industry," Roberto answered.

"Great, I am Toni. And you are?"

"I am Roberto," was the reply, embarrassed that she had formally done the introduction.

The following weeks saw Roberto and Toni spending every available minute of the day together. They went to ball games and regularly ate at the Piccolo Italia, where Roberto got ribbed from the family guys. He had become absolutely immersed in her company, as she was with him. They were literally inseparable, Roberto had met his future wife.

Roberto returned to England, with Toni as his wife, along with plans of escalating the business in the UK with the Rossi family. He had now learned his trade after three years in New York working for Benni.

On his return to England, Roberto and Giovanni took time to find and meet with factory owners who were producing munitions for the government. They found six factories that would suit the bill in the Manchester Trafford Park area. This area selected because it was the largest industrial estate in Europe and the brothers could easily disguise a small factory amongst the hundreds surrounding it.

The fourth person they met was Reggie Brown, a short, rotund character with a bald head with thick grey hair at the sides, with equally thick sideburns that rolled into a moustache. His double chin was cleanly shaven, which wobbled when he spoke. He was a single man who had never married but was always interested in the gadgets of the day.

He was angered at being told by the government that his successful luxury car supply business was to be used for the 'war effort' and that he must produce arms and munitions.

He owned the factory, which employed around one hundred men producing rifles from raw parts to the finished product. He ran a small foundry that could smelt the metal into the shapes required for the barrel, muzzle, trigger guard and bolt; he also utilised ten lathes turning parts for the guns. An outbuilding housed fourteen milling machines and eight boring machines, four were vertical and four horizontal. He had shaping machines, grinding machines, and three surface grinders. In addition to this, he had a small joinery shop that produced the wooden stocks and fore stocks for the guns.

The first meeting ended well and the subsequent meetings progressed even better. The final deal struck: all staff would be retained utilising their skills, and an immediate pay rise of one percent would be paid to keep them onside. Reggie was taking a good income of £9,000 per year. This would increase to £10,000 and he would become the new employed managing director. Besides, Roberto would pay Reggie £50,000 for the business and they would continue producing arms for the government for as long as the war running. Then, Roberto would find new markets. It was agreed, with a handshake, Roberto told Reggie that his solicitor, Daniel Davey, would draw up the necessary paperwork at no cost to Reggie.

On 8th May 1945, the Second World War ended. It was a war that neither Roberto nor Giovanni took part in, as there were no records of them existing, which meant the government could not recruit them.

Roberto was busy setting up markets to keep the employees of Brown's Engineering at work. He initially set up a deal with both sides of the Greek civil war, whilst quickly setting up deals for Poland and the Soviet Union versus the Partisans of the 1945-1947 conflict. The Indonesian Independence war of 1945-1946 quickly followed. The business started well.

CHAPTER EIGHTEEN.

Evening December 10^{th,} 1997

Seven Thirty came around soon enough. Jonty met with Jake in the hotel lobby. Jake was looking particularly nervous, They had been told to dress comfortably so they would have room to manoeuvre in their clothes if necessary. Jake wore a pair of his usual Levi 501's that were not too tight to allow freedom, a navy blue crew neck knotted Jumper with a white-collar over the neckline from the Fred Perry tee shirt he had under it. He was just putting his arm through a navy Barbour quilted coat, to keep the cold December weather at bay, as Jonty arrived.

"How are you feeling?" Jonty asked.

"I feel like a criminal, heading for a hit job," Jake replied.

"I know it's not ideal, but we need to do it this way to give Em a chance of getting out free and alive," Jonty responded.

Both men walked to the foyer of the hotel where Abano's men congregated.

The two BMWs they travelled from the jet in sat in the driveway of the hotel. This time, however, there was also a red, Mercedes Benz cargo van, the sprinter model.

Gus saw Jonty looking at the van and as usual, read his mind, "We chose red because white van drivers have a bad reputations here, as I guess they do in the UK." He slapped Jonty on the back and laughed.

'*How can he be so relaxed? I have never been that relaxed on any job on the force.*' Jonty thought.

As they left the hotel, the black night brightened by the deep orange clouds, which meant only one thing, snow was due.

They climbed into the BMWs, Jonty and Jake sat in the rear again with Gus riding in the front passenger seat, looking like his shoulders spread across most of the windscreen obscuring their view.

Jonty and Jake now knew who each of the team were, from a side view Jonty could make out that Piero was driving. Piero was looking very sixties in a pure white polo-neck jumper and a pair of sunglasses, they were not an asset as the daylight had been robbed a few hours ago.

As they drove into downtown Des Moines, Piero swung into Grand Avenue heading east. Jake looked out of the window, everything was happening in slow motion, they passed the art centre and greenwood park, people were milling around carrying shopping bags with Christmas logos on, they were smiling and happy all preparing for the onset of Christmas time.

Jake felt down, He thought of how only a few days ago He and Em were in South Story Street hunting down a large Christmas tree for the lounge.

The car continued before turning right onto water street, then left onto court avenue, within a few hundred yards and they were heading for the east side as the crossed the Des Moines River. Another left onto East Sixth Street, going over two more junctions, including Walnut Street. Jonty realised the zig-zagging of the streets was to put off any tracking that may be happening.

A final right into East Walden Street, the BMW decreased speed and came to a halt. Within seconds the following BMW pulled up behind followed by the Mercedes sprinter.

Jonty looked over the road, twenty yards away an Italian restaurant was well lit. A Christmas tree filled the window with multi-coloured lights twinkling off it. Larger Christmas lights were flashing around the sign for the restaurant. L'ULTIMA CENA.

The doors of the BMW's all opened simultaneously, Gus looked at the second car and put his thumbs-up, the sign that they were ready.

"Keep well to the rear of us." He told Jake and Jonty.

"And don't forget…."

"What we see must never be repeated." Jake interrupted.

"You got it," Gus replied.

Luca and Nani walked away from the cars before disappearing down a side street, their job was to enter from the rear.

Gus glanced down at his watch. He knew it would take around forty-five seconds to be in place, he allowed a minute, before nodding towards Luigi, Alessandro, and Piero to make their move towards the front door.

Not a word was spoken as they walked casually towards the door. Jonty could see Piero fully now he had a pair of dark chino's on with a smart Italian leather coat and a pair yellow caterpillar style boots on, all three looked more like lads having a relaxing night out, they began laughing and telling jokes to match the sight as they entered the door.

Alessandro patted Luigi on the back and said, "I swear to you that is the truth."

All three laughed, there was no story before the comment. It was all to look like relaxation, although deep within, none of them felt relaxed.

The waiter met them, "Can I help you sir?" he aimed his question at Piero.

"Yes, we have a table booked for three in the name of Abano."

The waiter nodded, "Yes sir, your table awaits." Abano was the password to direct them to the table designated. The table was square with plenty of room to enjoy a meal, there were four chairs around it. The cutlery was solid silver and it sat on a pristine white tablecloth.

The room had a high ceiling, the walls were painted lime green, the same shade as the olives grown back in Italy. The ceiling was white as Dean Martin sang 'It's beginning to look a lot like Christmas' gently through the high-quality speakers.

"And bring six bottles of bud, we are having a night out." Luigi half-shouted, acting a little drunk.

They sat four feet away from a table where three men sat, speaking quietly in unusual English accents, none of them were accustomed to the distinctive Liverpool accent.

On a table on the opposite side of the three Englishmen were a couple eating a starter of what looked like minestrone, this was Santi and Aria planted as the couple in the plan.

The waiter came over, as planned to the three Englishmen where he was to use the names they used to book the table. this would confirm to the Italians they were indeed the correct targets.

"How is everything, Mr. Fitzroy? Is it to your liking?" the waiter asked.

A reply came, in the strange English accent, "Everything is fine, thank you."

Success, all confirmed, they also now knew which one was Fitzroy, the toughest of the three.

The clock hit nine-thirty precisely, the time agreed to start the manoeuvres.

"Hey what did you say, did you just bad mouth my friend?" Piero pointed the question towards O'Neill.

O'Neill was halfway out of his seat, when Fitzroy put a hand on O'Neill's arm, "we don't need publicity," he whispered, O'Neill sat back down.

"I am sorry you must be mistaken, we were not speaking about you." Fitzroy correctly answered.

"I wasn't talking to you, I was talking to your coward friend sat next to you," Piero replied.

O'Neill's face distorted in anger, again Fitzroy put an arm on his friend.

"We do not want any trouble, let me buy you a drink and let's forget it ever happened," Fitzroy said, trying to placate the situation.

Luigi then entered the conversation, giving the impression he had been drinking a little too heavily. "You're not saying much are you a little afraid of us?"

The question aimed at Pitt, who had never backed down from anything in his life and was the Sartori hitman in his days before showing allegiance with Paul Jones.

Luigi turned to Piero and Alessandro. "The little English boys are afraid of us nice homely Italian boys." He laughed loudly, waving a bottle of Budweiser in the air and shuffling his feet as if unbalanced with too much alcohol.

Luigi goaded the three men. "There is wasteland right outside of this building, do any of you think you're tough enough to take me on?"

Steve Pitt's eyes narrowed menacingly, he never lost a fight and was tempted, but stayed quiet. He raised his head and looked at Luigi. Luigi had a squashed nose and a scar running across his right cheek to just under his eye, the scar tissue was a quarter of an inch wide in what had been a vicious attack.

The sight of Luigi's 'war wounds' would have feared most men, not Steve Pitt, he realised he had been on the wrong side of the arguments and would be warier of the people who put them there than Luigi receiving them. Pitt put his head back down.

Luigi threw his beer over Pitt, who glared at him and then looked at Fitzroy.

"OK, we don't follow them out, and you don't either." Looking at Piero and Alessandro.

"Fair enough," answered Piero.

"See you in five," Fitzroy told Pitt, with a wink. Pitt never lost, and Fitzroy knew, he had seen Pitt fight a hundred times.

Luigi and Pitt walked onto the waste ground, near an old building where nobody could see them.

Luigi started the fight with a right hook towards Pitt's head. Pitt put his forearm up to block the swing easily. Luigi then tried a left. Pitt easily stopped that too.

"You're out of your league here boy. You are going to get hurt." Pitt said in a menacing voice.

Luigi again tried to swing, this time he tried to hit Pitt hard and lost balance, Pitt hit Luigi in the stomach with an uppercut. Luigi bent with the pain before he knew it Pitt put his hands on the back of Luigi's head and pulled his head down, as he did he raised his right knee and smashed it into Luigi's face.

Luigi felt the familiar warm rush of blood, he knew there and then the nose was broken. As he tried to co-ordinate his feet, which were now wavering with short side to side steps, Pitt hit a right hook to Luigi's jaw, Luigi fell to the ground hurt and semi-conscious. Pitt had hit him hard, very hard.

Pitt kicked Luigi in the head and two teeth gave way, Luigi had the awareness to spit them out and not swallow.

Two bodies came out of the shadows, Gus and Paulo. Paulo hit Pitt across the side of the head with a baseball bat, Pitt half-turned, his strength amazed even Gus, but another strike on the back of the neck saw Pitt fall, Gus then jumped on Pitt's back and injected the anaesthetic he received from the hospital doctor. Pitt squirmed for a few seconds then lay prostrate on the ground. The two men who drove the Mercedes sprinter appeared, they were foot soldiers for the Mainiero family. Each had a duffle bag on their backs, both were dressed completely in black with black balaclavas and black gym shoes.

Freddie one of the foot soldiers took out a long piece of heavy rope and began tying Pitt from the ankles and connecting it to his wrists. They then carried him to the vacant Mercedes sprinter and deposited him in the back.

Ten Minutes passed, Fitzroy began to think where Pitt was, then, all of a sudden from the rear of the restaurant two men rushed in with hand-guns, shouting, "Everybody stays calm and nobody will get hurt!" All the fellow diners panicked. Suddenly, it became apparent to Fitzroy, they were being played.

Fitzroy went for his gun as did Luca, who had rushed from the rear with Nani, he pointed the gun at Fitzroy.

"Put the gun down Fitzroy, NOW!" Luca shouted.

Fitzroy did no such thing he fired at Luca hitting him square in the chest. The blood splattered the wall, a female diner sat next to the wall and screamed as Luca's blood ejected forcefully onto her Stella McCartney cream dress.

Before the smoke from the gun barrel disappeared Santi, who had been a passenger in the scene until now, left Aria's side and dived onto Fitzroy, just as Gus, Paulo,

Jonty, and Jake entered the room. Fitzroy was surprised and lost balance. Gus ran over and quickly injected the second syringe into his neck and watched him slide slowly to the floor.

"What is going on here?" O'Neill, the remaining one of the Fitzroy party, shouted.

"You don't need to know," Paulo answered.

Piero, Santi, Alessandro, and Nani all surrounded O'Neill. Gus approached from behind. The third anaesthetic delivered.

Freddie and his working mate, Jim 'Boy' Smithson, loaded the dead weight bodies of Fitzroy and O'Neill into the sprinter, along with Luca, who was killed with the single-shot off Fitzroy.

They helped Luigi into one of the BMWs, he was hurt badly from the fight with Pitt, but still had the energy to ask a question.

"Gus, why did you let the fight go so long with Pitt?"

Gus replied, "Because I wanted to see if he was as good as Jonty had told me, and he was."

They drove the cars and sprinter into the night with, one dead team member, one badly injured, and three unconscious bodies.

"All in a day's work," Gus told Jonty.

CHAPTER NINETEEN.

MANCHESTER 1947.

January 1, 1947, saw the Nationalisation of Britain's coal industry. Mining communities believed this marked the winning of an epic struggle for decent wages security and public ownership of a vital resource.

On Vesting Day, miners and their families marched in their thousands behind banners and colliery bands to the pitheads. They cheered and some openly wept, as the blue and white flag of the National Coal Board was unfurled above them. They crowded around the unveiled plaques which proclaimed:

'This colliery is now managed by the National Coal Board on behalf of the people.'

The dawn of nationalisation brought hope to the miners who lived with the evils of privately owned pits all their lives. One could almost hear the cheers of heroes and heroines from the past and present celebrating the reality of public ownership.

Stood on the side-lines watching the events unfold was a young parish priest who had nothing but the community of his parish at his heart. The twenty-five old priest stood with pride as the people rejoiced in a changing world from the powerful pit owners, who would always put profit before safety or the wellbeing of the miners who risked life and limb to fill the ever-deepening pockets of the wealthy greedy owners. Nationalisation will allow the government to look after the wellbeing of all mining communities.

Two years earlier, on a wet March day in nineteen-forty five, one of the six thousand strong parish population of St Theresa's church came to see father Matthew Fitzpatrick. He offered Father Fitzpatrick help and assistance to help his community achieve better working conditions.

Fitzpatrick thought back to that day as the people celebrated and danced in the streets in front of him. He thought how he sat in his office preparing the sermon to be read the following Sunday at mass.

***

Manchester, March 1945.

A knock rattled the door. "Come in!" shouted Father Fitzpatrick

A man walked into the door, he had a grey overcoat on which was wet from the persistent rain that had fallen over the last twenty-four hours. The man had a big smile on his face.

"Hello, Father I hope I am not disturbing you."

"Not at all please come in, Take your coat off, it is dripping with rain."

The man took his coat off and underneath was a very expensive looking grey suit; he wore it with a crisp white shirt complementing a grey and navy tie. He had expensive leather shoes that were the rain globules sat as bubbles on the top, no water would penetrate these shoes. As he handed the overcoat to the priest, he also took off a wet grey trilby hat with a navy band around it.

This man protrudes wealth, Fitzpatrick thought as his first impression made him smile.

"Father, thank you for seeing me, my name is Giovanni Sartori, I am a parishioner and I thought I could help both the parish and yourself, by arranging stability in our much-loved community." Giovanni opened.

"I am listening." the priest responded.

Giovanni began to talk to Father Matthew Fitzpatrick.

"Twenty years ago in 1926 there was a happening that shook the very foundations of British capitalism, of which our parish was part of, the British working class moved into action in the general strike of twenty-six. For nine days, from, the third of May, not a wheel turned nor a light shone without the permission of the working class. In such a moment, with such power, surely it ought to have been possible to have transformed society?"

Giovanni took a sip from his tea the priest had ordered for them both from Mrs. Doherty, his housekeeper, before continuing. "How can such a position have ended in defeat?" The priest looked at him still unsure where this conversation was going.

"If the strike did not make the desired change meant by the working class, and it didn't! I saw this as a weakness in the working class and I would like to support our parish with your help Father."

Father Fitzpatrick looked impressed as he took a long deep breath, before answering, "What do you have in mind, Mr. Sartori?"

"Giovanni, please Father."

Giovanni picked up the direction again, "The UK had experienced industrial stagnation, since then with the pit owners keeping the miners in dangerous occupations and wages low whilst illness and disease was common in all working communities. This was particularly marked in the UK Coal Industry, of which the majority of our parish was, and still are, employed.

The declining industry led to increasingly bitter trade disputes, this culminated in the general strike. The miners went on strike for better pay, and working conditions, they were joined by some other trade unions. However, the general strike was only partial and led to the defeat of the miners, during the strike, the middle class enthusiastically filled in for jobs helping to break the strike and increase a sense of class and social division. My brother and I took the view to throw our support behind the working class, and our parish." This received a nod of appreciation.

Giovanni continued, "In two years the government will nationalise the coal industry until then we intend to support the employees for a further two years."

"I entirely agree that the parish could do with support for the strong working-class mining community we have! What I fail to see is how I as the parish priest can help?"

"That is why I am here today Father, We entered agreements with both the Unions and the mine owners many years ago to protect the wellbeing of the employed staff, we intend to honour that agreement. All we ask from you Father is support and a word in the appropriate ears as and when the time is required. We would also support you and the church funds handsomely!"

Giovanni chose his target well, he knew that Father, Matthew Fitzpatrick had been brought up on the tough streets of Manchester and that he was no stranger to crime and violence, before entering the church he had been convicted and sentenced in Strangeways prison for grievous bodily harm on no other than three men at the same time singlehanded!

"That's all you want me to do?" asked the priest.

"That is all," answered Giovanni "I am sure the Bishop above you will see kindly on the very high contributions that will be going through the church funds. Indeed a word into the correct ears could even see a promotion for you."

A month passed before the first assignment for Father Matthew. David Johnson, an ex-local pit owner, stood outside the church one Sunday arguing with a few miners about the salary they were receiving, he told them that they were lucky to be getting the pittance of a wage they were receiving, and the fact that it was a free labour market should they want to leave. Aware they would not be able to find labour in the tight times found themselves in.

David Johnson was later found dead after an 'apparent horse riding accident'. Roberto told all the owners he was a fair man and that for the sum of two thousand guineas each per month, which equated to an annual income of twenty-six thousand four hundred pounds per pit. He promised not to charge each pit at a different fee, guaranteeing equal rights.

Johnson had been missing payments and told Roberto he had no intention of paying.

"Many years have passed since the general strike, we do not risk anymore, and even if the workers did strike we have all built enough funds to survive. Your usefulness is now defunct!" Johnson had told Roberto.

Giovanni and his foot soldiers managed this operation. The twenty-four pits brought a gross annual income of £633,000, the outgoings consisted of putting the five most influential union leaders on two thousand pounds per year retainer.

The rumours following Johnson's death were rife Roberto, Giovanni, and Father Matthew were seen as modern-day martyrs fighting the cause of the working class, they had all earned a significant amount of money from their efforts and large sums were being donated to St Theresa's, a point that was not missed by the hierarchy in the Manchester diocese.

Father Matthew Fitzpatrick sold himself to the Sartori family a contract he would be reminded of many times in the future!

CHAPTER TWENTY

December 11th, 1997

The convoy of two five series BMW's and the red Mercedes sprinter entered the gates of an industrial unit on the outskirts of town. It drove to the very edge where a large warehouse sat. It was fifty yards away from the nearest building, which was an engineering company and was always noisy with the sound of machinery.

Nino, jumped out of the BMW he had been travelling in, looked around to check how many people were around, none, it was a quarter to midnight with heavy snow falling, perfect to keep people in their homes.

He walked up to the large navy painted sliding doors, took a key from his pocket, unlocked the doors, and slid them open.

The cars and sprinter drove slowly through the doors and into the warehouse, Nino, slid the doors shut locked them up again before switching on the lights.

Jonty could see that it was very basic, it was brick-walled with a corrugated roof, possibly asbestos from the age it looked, it was a dirty grey, the years had weathered it. He noticed it had no windows, only skylights in the roof, on the far end of the building was a set of offices, they looked unused along with a building that he assumed was the lavatory.

He continued to look around, he could see six beds on wheels, similar to the type used in hospitals along with a few workbenches with vices attached to them there were also a few old pillar drills and basic engineering machines, lathes, and milling machines.

"First things first," Gus said, his voice echoed in the vast emptiness the warehouse provided.

"Get the three bodies on the beds and strapped. I want the back of the beds hinged up to as near a sitting position as is possible, and make sure when they come round they can't move." Gus Ordered.

"Whilst the lads are doing that Freddie, I want you to take Luca's body to the other end of the warehouse and dispose of it as you normally would."

At the other end of the one hundred yard building stood a large furnace, obviously used to make people 'disappear' when required. Freddie nodded, climbed into the sprinter, then drove it to the other end of the building. He fired up the furnace.

"That's it lads no more work to do until the morning, let us all get some sleep," Gus said as he nodded to a door about halfway down the warehouse.

They entered it, an annexe that had five rooms leading off it. All the doors were open, Jonty could see three large bedrooms each with two single beds, a bathroom with a shower and a lounge-type area, large enough for a three-piece suite a TV and a small kitchen unit with cooking facilities, a fridge and a freezer, Gus walked up to the fridge and took a bud out.

"Help yourself," he said to Jonty and Jake.

Jonty replied, "I think I need to sleep more than eat food or a drink, where am I sleeping?"

Gus gestured by pointing his beer bottle towards a room. "You and Jake take up in there for the night."

Jonty woke early the next morning with the sound of heavy doors opening. He climbed out of bed and nudged Jake from slumber.

He had a quick shower as the other men were also coming around from the noise. Jonty showered and dressed. Jake was in a queue for the bathroom. Jonty strolled through to the warm warehouse, he looked down to see Freddie and Jim Boy working around the furnace, there was a bright orange glow which silhouetted the two men as black figures, He saw them swing open the rear doors of the sprinter and bring out a long shape in a sack. This was Luca.

He watched on as Freddie and Jim Boy struggled to lift Luca, they placed the body on a trolley and waited.

As Jonty watched, he heard a voice shout "Ball what are, you doing here?"

Jonty turned to see Fitzroy, sat at an angle of about seventy degrees, the maximum the bed allowed, he, was tied and handcuffed to the rails of the bed, unable to move.

"Who wants to know?" Jonty sarcastically replied.

"Seeing you makes me understand now, It's about the Hughes woman isn't it?"

"You went a step too far kidnapping her," Jonty replied.

Fitzroy laughed and spat on the floor.

By this time, Gus and the men had entered the room.

"You and Jake join us at the bottom of the building Jonty," Gus asked.

They all strolled down, quietly towards the furnace, when they arrived, Luca was lay on one of the spare hospital beds, cleaned up as best as Freddie and Jim boy could do.

They all gathered around Luca's body.

Gus clasped his hands and bowed his head, the other men followed suit.

Gus took a minute to wipe a tear away, "Luca was a good man, I knew him since he was around five or six. He has given his life to helping a young woman we will find and return safely. I promise you, Luca, your life will not disappear in vain."

Gus then said a prayer out loud.

"God our Father,
Your power brings us to birth,
Your providence guides our lives,
and by Your command, we return to dust.

Lord, those who die still live in Your presence,
their lives change but do not end.
I pray in hope for my family,
relatives, and friends,
and for all the dead known to You alone.

In company with Christ,
Who died and now lives,
may they rejoice in Your kingdom,
where all our tears are wiped away.
Unite us together again in one family,
to sing Your praise forever and ever.
Amen."

"He got all he deserved." a voice came from the other end of the room. It was O'Neill.

Gus ignored the comment although Alessandro, who was Luca's close friend, visibly clenched his teeth and tightened up in his shoulders.

Gus looked at Alessandro and gave a slight shake of the head, "Bide your time Alli," Gus whispered.

Freddie and Jim boy, then walked up to Luca's body, Freddie stood at the head, Jim to the feet, and between them, they lifted the body and swung it, hammock-style,

Freddie counted, "One, two, three!" On three, they released their hold as the body entered the furnace. First Luca's clothes began to burn then the sight of melting flesh, the dark smoke of burning oils from the body could be seen. The body began to crackle and sizzle. The flames engulfed the carcass as if a shoal of piranha were devouring it. After a few minutes the flames rescinded, Jonty looked in the furnace again, he could see the bones from Luca's skull, neck and shoulders; they sat on top of the red-hot glowing coals.

It was the Abano family's way to cremate any of their family or soldiers privately if killed in action. It kept risk and publicity low.

"We have work to do," Gus said as he began walking with a long quick stride back up the warehouse concrete floor, away from the furnace, in the direction of Fitzroy, Pitt, and O'Neill.

"Who is the strongest, who is the toughest and who is the one most likely to crack?" Gus asked Jonty, in a low voice.

"Fitzroy is mentally the strongest, Pitt is the toughest and O'Neill would be the most vulnerable," Jonty replied in an equally low voice.

CHAPTER TWENTY-ONE

Manchester 1947

"Father Matthew, are you in the living world?" Giovanni joked with the priest.

"Yes, sorry Giovanni, I was away with my thoughts," as he snapped out of thinking about the first visit from Giovanni two years earlier.

Father Matthew's housekeeper brought in a tray of hot coffee, Mrs. Doherty liked Giovanni, and the best freshest biscuits or cake, were always delivered in his presence, today it was digestive biscuits. She had made coffee, espresso-style for Giovanni, and an American white for Father Matthew.

"You look wet, Giovanni, I have made a nice warm fire, when I knew you were coming on such an awful day," Mrs. Doherty said.

"Thank you, Mrs. Doherty, that will be all for now," Father Matthew replied.

"I was just thinking of when you first came to the house, Giovanni and you asked me a favour, you have asked for several since I assume today is no different?" Father Matthew asked.

"As you know father Mathew I am on very friendly terms with Archbishop O'Dea, I hope you don't mind but your name came up in conversation." Giovanni began, before selecting a Digestive from the plate Mrs. Doherty had left.

Father Matthew listened intensely to Giovanni.

"I told him what a fabulous job you are doing in the parish and your heart is always based at the centre of the community, the workers."

"Thank you, Giovanni, it is appreciated." Father Matthew replied.

Giovanni continued, "He commented on how well you raise funds and was impressed by the upkeep of St Theresa's."

Thank you Giovanni, but it is the kind hearts of you and Roberto who funds the vast majority of funding." Father Matthew said.

"You are too kind Father Matthew," Giovanni took a sip of coffee and a bite of his biscuit, he was a master at building hope in people, and that is what he was doing here with Father Matthew by taking a second or two out of the conversation.

"I am not sure if you are aware, Father Matthew, but a vacancy for the role of a new bishop has risen in this diocese."

"I had heard on the grapevine," Father Matthew replied.

"Well Father Matthew, The archbishop told me if you could generate a further twenty thousand pounds for the diocese, the job would be yours."

"Twenty thousand is a lot to raise Giovanni, I assume you have a plan?"

"You are ahead of your time Father Matthew, I do have a plan that will raise exactly £20,000." The two men smiled at each other. A smile only made with full trust in each other.

"Tell me more Giovanni?"

"We recently bought a factory in Trafford Park, we initially bought it as an ammunition factory to help with the war effort, you know we all have to do our bit father." They both laughed.

"Indeed," Father Matthew replied.

"We kept the factory running because three hundred plus people are working there and, as you know father, we protect the working class." Father Matthew nodded.

"One person, however, is trying to disrupt our, let's say generosity, towards employment." Giovanni ended.

"It must be an important task if you are willing to donate twenty thousand pounds, Giovanni?" Father Matthew asked.

Giovanni replied, "Sometimes humans must risk their lives to accept what is best for other humans, as Jesus did on the cross to save humanity."

Father Matthew asked, "Who is this person? Who must be sacrificed?"

"Gerald Hesketh."

"Gerald Hesketh! As in Gerald Hesketh the member of parliament?" Father Matthew asked.

"You know him then?" Giovanni teased.

"Any specific time scale?" Father Matthew asked.

"Let us say in the next month or so before the vacancy is filled," was the reply.

Gerald Hesketh had requested a meeting with Roberto and Giovanni two months earlier, which was accepted, they met at Manchester town hall in an office used by Hesketh.

The town hall was a very impressive building, it sat in a square called, Albert square, named after Queen Victoria's husband, Prince Albert who died of typhoid in 1861.

Within the square there is a memorial in the memory of Prince Albert, It features a marble statue of Albert standing on a plinth and facing west, designed by Matthew

Noble. The figure sits within a large Medieval-style ciborium designed by the architect Thomas Worthington. Noble was commissioned by the then-mayor, Thomas Goadsby, to sculpt the Prince's likeness, the design was personally approved by Queen Victoria.

As Roberto and Giovanni entered the impressive building, the large entrance was lined by statues of famous, Manchester historic people.

John Dalton the famous English chemist best known for introducing the atomic theory into chemistry, and for his research into colour blindness, sometimes referred to as Daltonism in his honour.

James Prescott Joule, physicist, mathematician, and brewer, born in Salford, Lancashire. Joule studied the nature of heat. The SI derived unit of energy, the joule, named after him.

Roberto and Giovanni walked past the statues in the great hall and many others, all of the people who had contributed to the world from Manchester or Salford backgrounds.

They walked towards the stairs on the tiled floors where many bees where skilfully tiled in mosaic., this is a tribute to the working people of Manchester, who over the years, built and operated in the working capital of the world during the industrial revolution.

They walked up the stairs and under the gothic arch-shaped ceilings made in stone and past the meeting rooms where original large paintings hung on the walls, to a small office at the end of the hallway. They knocked on the door.

"Enter," a voice said from the other side of the door.

Roberto and Giovanni entered.

The room was small, possibly twelve feet square, it was decorated basically. There were wooden floorboards, a high ceiling, painted white along with white walls, a bookcase stretched along one wall, full of books about Manchester past. Roberto noticed one with Peterloo written down the spine.

"Sit down Gentlemen," said the man behind the small but adequate desk in the corner of the room. "I would offer you coffee but I haven't got a lot to say so you won't be here long." It was Gerald Hesketh M.P. speaking.

Giovanni and Roberto discussed many years ago how to deal with this type of situation, they had agreed, do not change your facial expression, do not look at each other and do not take your eyes off the person who is speaking. They both carried it out to the letter.

Hesketh in return meant to make an impact. He coughed and squirmed in his seat a little when he saw two motionless, expressionless, people sat opposite him.

"Gentlemen," he continued, "It has been brought to my attention that you own a factory in Trafford Park, is this correct?"

No emotion or change from Giovanni or Roberto.

"OK let me ask another way," Hesketh said, "I know you have a factory in Trafford Park."

No emotion,

"I am also led to believe that you are continuing to make ammunition, but nobody knows where you are selling it. Is it legal?"

Nothing from Roberto or Giovanni.

"Again then gentlemen, I will tell you, what you need to do. You will bring me your accounts showing me every customer you do business with and a full inventory of your business. Do you understand?"

Nothing from Roberto and Giovanni,

"I know legally you don't have to show me, but something does not smell right about your business, there will be no stone unturned as I find out about your company and I will expose you for what you are. CRIMINALS!"

Roberto and Giovanni both stood in unison and walked out of the door as one.

***

Father Matthew chose his night well. His criteria was to do it before the 26th March, when daylight hours extended because of the clocks going forward, he chose the 15th March, as it also meant not as many police would be on the streets as the police were holding their annual ball, which Roberto and Giovanni were attending, following large donations throughout the year.

Father Matthew left the rectory under the cover of darkness at eight in the evening precisely; he walked the two miles to the part of the parish he was going to randomly drop in on a few parishioners.

By eight twenty, He reached his first destination. He was dressed in his usual all-black attire with a black Abercrombie overcoat and black leather gloves. He had a black trilby hat, helping keep the steady cold, moderate rain from his face, he was also carrying a black umbrella. To cover his clothing

The rain kept people off the streets, an advantage for this night's work.

He arrived at his first call and knocked on the door. The door opened "Father, how good to see you. I would have made you a meal or something."

"Thank you but I am just making a few 'on the spot' calls to people in the parish."

He unfolded his umbrella and shook it before entering the Victorian building, there was a small hallway, with coats hung up on the left. The tiles were classic period set in a black and white alternating design. He took his overcoat off and shuddered as if releasing the cold and wet from his body.

He was invited into the lounge where the fire was raging in the middle of the twenty-foot, room, he sat on a comfortable chair in front of the fire and was offered a cup of tea which he gratefully accepted.

Five minutes later Gerald Hesketh walked into the room, with a tray along with a china teapot and two matching china cups on board.

"What a pleasure it is to see you, Father, how are you doing?"

"I am doing well thanks Gerald, I haven't seen you at mass recently and I just wanted to see that you are OK."

"How kind of you to be so interested Father thank you, I have been busy lately what with travelling to Westminster and working on local issues and so on."

"What are the local issues Gerald, anything I should be aware of?"

"Not really father, I have an issue with two rogues in Trafford Park, but nothing I can't handle and certainly nothing I need to worry you about."

The opportunity soon came that Father Matthew had been waiting for. "Excuse me father, the old bladder isn't as strong as it once was." Hesketh left the room to relieve himself.

Father Matthew reached into his pocket and pulled out a small bottle with a Kilner clasped lid on it securing its contents.

Giovanni organised, from people on the payroll, in Manchester Royal Hospital, a portion of Romeo. It was called such as, a code name but its contents were the same as the poison Romeo took in the famous Shakespear play.

The drug is best known for being a fast-acting poison. An obvious choice for such a strong poison is potassium cyanide or the medieval monkshood, both of which cause rapid respiratory failure, Giovanni had selected the potassium cyanide, as it was readily available to medical staff.

Father Matthew went to the drinks cupboard in the corner of the living room and poured two Glenfiddich whisky's, he knew it was Hesketh's favourite drink.

On Hesketh's, return Father Matthew said, "I felt I needed warming up Gerald, so I took the liberty of pouring two glasses of whisky, I hope you don't mind."

"Mind, it's a fantastic idea, Father."

Father Matthew handed one, with the poison in, to Hesketh, knowing the whiskey would mask the background taste.

"Down the hatch," Father Matthew said and drank his without a pause.

"Down the hatch," Hesketh replied, feeling obliged to follow Father Matthew in drinking it in one.

Within minutes, Hesketh felt drowsy, "Let me get you comfortable Gerald, you look tired." He placed him on a chair near the window, opened the curtains, and left the lights on.

Father Matthew waited another ten minutes making sure Hesketh was unconscious at best, during the ten minutes, he washed the teacups and his empty whisky glass before placing it back in the drinks cabinet, He left the property, through the front door, and at no time did he take his gloves off.

Father Matthew's next move was to visit around half a dozen parishioners around the area. An hour and a half later he was leaving Mrs. McGovern's house, which was next door but one to Hesketh. He wished Mrs. McGovern a good evening and walked away from the house.

Two minutes later he knocked back on the door of Mrs. McGovern, she opened it.

"Hello Father you look flustered, is everything alright?"

"I am not sure Mrs. McGovern. As you know I have been doing my routine visits. On leaving you I went to see Mr. Hesketh, however, when I knocked on the door there was no answer, I noticed there was a light on, I went to look, Mr. Hesketh was sat in a chair, at first I thought he was asleep, I knocked very hard on the window and still no response. I am worried. Could I use your phone to call the police?"

The police turned up within thirty minutes, Father Matthew stayed in Mrs. McGovern's home to wait. She made him a cup of tea to calm his nerves. PC North walked in the house and shook hands with Father Matthew.

"Hello father, can you tell me what happened?" North asked.

Matthew relayed the story from leaving Mrs. McGovern's house.

"He left here officer and within two minutes he was back asking could he use the telephone?"

A perfect alibi thought father Matthew.

An inquiry followed, the result was suicide by poison, the perfect murder.

Within three days, Father Matthew received a cheque for the parish for twenty thousand pounds.

Within seven days Father, Matthew was invited to an interview with Archbishop O'Dea for the vacant Bishop position, in the Manchester diocese.

Within ten days Father Matthew received a letter from Archbishop to confirm he was successful in his application

Within half an hour of the confirmation letter arriving, Father Matthew's telephone rang. He answered it.

"Congratulations on your new position bishop Fitzpatrick, a well-earned promotion." The familiar voice of Giovanni Sartori spoke at the end of the line.

Bishop Fitzpatrick, that sounds just fantastic. Bishop Fitzpatrick thought.

CHAPTER TWENTY-TWO.

December 12^{th,} 1997

 Gus, Jonty, Jake, and the team arrived at the other end of the warehouse, Fitzroy's face filled with anger. His eyes were bulging with rage, teeth clenched. He began to growl. Like a dog tied up on a chain.
 Pitt and O'Neill were also showing anger. Pitt was slavering at the mouth and had no free hand to wipe it away. All three men felt caged and ineffective.
 "Good morning gentlemen. I am not going to hold you responsible for the death of my very good friend, Luca, as I know you were doing your job as we were doing ours."
 "Do you need others to do your job Ball? Have you gone soft?" Pitt goaded Jonty.
 Jonty looked back, smiled, before replying: "Long time Steve. I have never seen you look better."
 He continued, "When was the last time we met? Don't tell me let me guess, ah I have it, at Paul Jones house, he had a helicopter ride as I remember." referring to the day His superior masterminded Paul Jones's escape.
 Jonty told the story to Gus and his men.
 "I was at a shotgun scene at Billy Jones's house, the day Quinn helped Billy escape, that's correct isn't, it boys?" He looked at Fitzroy and Pitt.

"Then, out of the blue a voice came through the microphone in the white van I was sitting in, it was my boss Superintendent Quinn."

"Hello, Inspector Lee and Detective Inspector Ball, Quinn said to me and my colleague."

"Hello, sir!" we replied in unison.

"You are doing a grand job there," Quinn said. "I have been discussing with an emergency action team about how is the best way to handle this situation." Jonty continued the story as the room listened.

"I had never heard of an emergency action team, however, he was my superior."

"Keep it quiet down there," Quinn asked me. He then went on to add, "I will let you know when we have a plan formulated."

"The speaker in the van came to life again with Quinn's voice, a little later.

Afternoon, both, I assume all is the same? I have not heard from you?"

"Yes, sir, I responded, feeling like a naughty schoolboy for not having reported anything.

"We have a plan," Quinn told me. "I have ordered a helicopter with armed marksmen on board to land in Billy Jones' garden. They will attack the house to minimise fatalities, as the situation currently is like a powder keg."

Lee, my colleague for the day, did not seem happy with this. "Have my line agreed to this, sir?"

"Yes!" was Quinn's reply. "I have just left the meeting. Do you have a problem?"

"No, sir."

"Expect the helicopter in the next fifteen minutes." Quinn signed off.

Lee turned to Jonty. "This does not make sense at all."

Jonty shrugged his shoulders. "Ours is not to question why," was his response.

"Let the team on the ground know what to expect," he told Ged, his aide who was co-ordinating the operation.

"Yes, sir," replied Ged.

He wasted no time in telling the armed team to spread throughout the grounds, to expect a helicopter and they must make crossfire to protect their colleagues in the chopper.

Fifteen minutes, as promised by Quinn, the distant unmistakable sound of helicopter rotors came into earshot, slowly increasing in volume as it neared the house. It came into view, first as a speck on the shortened horizon, then slowly becoming larger with the unmistakable dark blue body with a yellow top and yellow lettering reading 'POLICE' under the side windows.

The Euro copter EC-145 helicopter eased its way over the top of the house and spinning in a circular motion, while the pilot looked for a safe landing place.

The helicopter landed behind the house, unseen by the eye, but a camera in the van picked up the details. Lee and Jonty watched in fascination as the chopper touched down and three armed officers exited the machine, sprinting towards the house. One of the officers was carrying a rope. He tied one end to the door handle on the back door of the house, the other end he tied to the helicopter's left-hand landing skid.

The helicopter rose slightly off the ground and flew a few yards further away from the house. The door flew off its hinges in seconds, the jamb coming with it. As the officers ran into the house, they saw flashing coming through the windows, a sure sign of gunfire.

"Something doesn't seem right here!" Lee said to Jonty. "That entrance was too easy and not textbook."

As soon as Lee said it, one officer came out of the house with Billy and Maggie. Both were handcuffed, their hands behind their backs, and a gun pointed at them. They were shunted into the helicopter. The other officer climbed in after them, slashing the rope attached to the now fragmented back door. The doors to the helicopter slid shut and it lifted off the ground. As it climbed, the order to ceasefire adhered to.

Lee again spoke up. "Something is not right." He frowned. "The Euro copter EC-145 seats nine people. If they planned to capture two prisoners, why not have a team of seven for maximum safety? Instead, there are only three, plus a pilot, making four, it just does not add up. I decided to go down to the house and take a look for myself" Jonty continued.

"I am coming with you," Lee said to Jonty.

Jonty nodded nervously and both men walked towards the house. The copper beech stood there in all its glory. Its leaves lay spread on the autumn lawn, glistening in the relentless November drizzle. The two officers walked through the half-open gates. They strode down the gravel path, the stones crunching beneath their feet.

They continued to walk around the back of the house to the hole in the wall, which, five minutes previously, had been the back door. They walked through to see holes in the ceiling where bullets had penetrated. On the floor in front of them lay the two officers, riddled with bullets. The tell-tale signs of the bullet entry indicated that the shots had come from the back door area, which instantly told Jonty that it must have been the leaving officer who shot his unsuspecting colleagues.

"We have been stitched up like kippers," Jonty said. "It was a plan to get Billy out. The holes in the ceiling were a decoy to make us think a gun battle was taking place. While they were shooting the ceiling to bits, probably Billy, the last one was putting the handcuffs on Maggie and then finally Billy. They left for the helicopter making it look like Billy was being arrested. There was just enough time for them to make their getaway."

Jonty ended the story.

"And so started the great escape for Billy Jones and My superintendent, John Quinn."

"Of course," Jonty started up again, "This then led to bank assets being frozen, Paul Jones owing millions to South American drug barons and no money to pay them. He looked at Fitzroy. They stared into each other's eyes for a minute.

Jonty continued "Enter the three musketeers, But instead of Athos, Porthos and Aramis, we have Fitzroy, Pitt, and O'Neill."

Gus smiled at the analogy.

Jonty, continued, "So a nice easy job, kidnap Emily Hughes, blackmail her wealthy father and all is done, easy."

Well, lads, you hit a problem. The gentleman on my right, is called Gus Abano, you may have heard of the Abano family?"

"Now the Abano family are very friendly with the Mainiero family, you may have heard of them too?" Jonty made a gesture to his left "May I introduce you to Paulo Conchetti."

Paulo spoke, "It's a pleasure Gentlemen."

If Fitzroy had not understood what was happening he was beginning to understand the gravity of the situation at this point.

Fitzroy spoke, aiming it at Gus. "Why are you siding with a copper? We are family we are the Sartori Family, who before that were the Rossi Family, we are family."

Gus looked at Fitzroy, who had an expensive pair of dark Armani jeans and a navy Fred Perry tee shirt on, badly stained and torn at the sleeve, following the previous evening's events.

"Well, Ken. Is it ok if I call you Ken?" Gus asked in a very low deep voice, Gus's voice reminded Jonty of Barry White singing.

Gus continued, "As I see it the minute Don Paul Jones, the Sartori godfather, attempted to murder Giovanni Sartori at Roberto's funeral, then succeeded in killing a family friend and a religious man, Archbishop Matthew Fitzpatrick. This Ken was the moment all the other families spat on Paul Jones." Gus looked evil now the rage of Luca was rising in his throat.

"We recognise Giovanni as the Don Giovanni and we will support him, as we would any family member," Gus concluded.

Jonty picked it up again, "As you can see lads you have a problem, you have a chance of resolving this if you answer two questions."

"Which are?" Fitzroy asked, with his already strong Liverpool accent strengthening.

"One: You tell us where Emily is so we can bring her back safely," Jonty answered.

"Two: You tell us where Quinn and Jones are?"

Fitzroy laughed hard. He laughed so hard his stomach pressed into the tight leather strap around his waist and under the bed keeping him pinned, His wrists tied tightly, with thick rope, as were his ankles. A longer piece of rope connected his wrists to his feet, His wrists and ankles were also clamped by four sets of handcuffs, one for each limb, attached to the metal frame of the bed. Pitt and O'Neill both tied identically.

"Do you think I will give you that information? I will take the beating now and keep quiet."

"It wasn't a beating we had in mind," Gus answered. He nodded to Alessandro.

Alessandro walked towards the kitchen.

"Luca and Alessandro were the best of friends," Gus paused "I am sorry you don't know who they are, do you?"

Gus paused again, before continuing "Allisandro, is the man who has just walked away, and Luca, is the man you shot in the chest last night, who is also the man you saw going in the furnace after being murdered by you, they were the closest of friends, since childhood."

Alessandro returned with a normal household item. A steam iron, the iron was of normal shape, square at the bottom, straight up the sides for around five inches then tapering to an apex at the end of the plate.

Alessandro plugged the iron into a wall socket.

"Set it on level two," Gus told Alessandro.

"Now Ken, where is Emily?" Gus asked.

Fitzroy spat at Gus, Freddie and Jim Boy stood at the end of Pitt's bed, Gus nodded. Freddie wheeled the bed to within reach of the steam iron.

Alessandro had a knife in his hand. He cut Pitt's Levi 501's from the waist down to the knee on the right side.

"Where is Emily?" Gus asked Fitzroy again.

"Go to hell!" was the reply.

Alessandro lifted Pitt's black boxer shorts slightly.

"Only to the count of three Alli," Gus ordered Alessandro.

Alessandro placed the iron on Pitt's thigh and counted to three slowly.

Pitt screamed, his head shook violently grey putrid steam came from the leg, the smell of oil being evaporating from the skin smelt like burning rubber.

Alli smiled at Gus, this would be his revenge for Luca.

Pitt was cursing and had no way of helping the pain. He could not put it underwater or rub it as he lay motionless, except for a writhing head jerking on a left to right axis violently. "When I get free from this your life won't be worth living, trust me on that!" He screamed.

"Where is Emily?" Gus asked Fitzroy, "It's your turn next."

Fitzroy never spoke, he just smiled. "Well done Steve, it will take more than these to break us eh!" he shouted over to Pitt.

Gus shouted over to Alessandro again. "Level six Alli."

Freddie wheeled Pitt away, Pit still screaming violently, Jonty looked at his thigh, a deep red imprint of the steam irons base that looked redraw.

Freddie then wheeled Fitzroy to the position Pitt vacated. This time the iron was steaming and hissing on the side.

"Where is Emily?" Gus asked again,

No reply,

"Count to seven Alli," Gus told Alessandro.

Again, the same process, a knife slashing the jeans, this time though they were very expensive Armani jeans.

"Where is Emily?" Gus asked in his low drawl.

"In hell where she belongs," Fitzroy's replied.

Alessandro, smiled, he was glad Fitzroy had not told Gus. This was going to be sweet revenge for the man who killed Luca.

Alessandro placed the iron on Fitzroy's thigh, now on the top setting, of six.

He pressed hard, not light as he had with Pitt.

Fitzroy screamed at the intense pain. Thick grey smoke billowed from the flesh as the iron penetrated,

Jonty instinctively turned and heaved as the hot putrid smell of burning flesh entered his nostrils.

Alessandro continued to smile, he counted slowly, taking ten seconds to count to seven.

Fitzroy had never experienced pain like it. He could smell his own burning, melting, oozing, disintegrating flesh.

"That's long enough Alli," Gus shouted.

Alessandro began lifting the iron, at first it stuck as the melted flesh welded to Fitzroy's leg.

Alessandro yanked the iron away, string-like skin stretched from the base of the iron to the leg, Alessandro pulled it harder to release the iron from the ever expanding skin.

The iron took every layer of skin away, there was a semi-fluid glue textured burn the shape of the iron, as the skin wept spots appeared in front of their eyes. Blood trickled out slowly rather than spurted. Veins were showing, some burnt through and some straggling. Sinews were melting and an inch of thighbone was visible, Alessandro had gone deeper than Gus had seen before when using the steam iron torture, or the "SIT and beg" as they called it.

Jake looked on, the scene reminded him of adverts used to tempt people into buying pizza. A slice of pizza is lifted from the main pizza portion in slow motion, the mozzarella stretches from the pizza, finally it breaks away and the cheese snaps back. Jake replaced the scene in his minds-eye, the main part of the Pizza was now replaced with Fitzroy's thigh, the triangular piece replaced by the steam iron, and finally, the stretching, stringy, mozzarella replaced by the skin.

Fitzroy passed out after around three seconds. Alessandro delivered first-degree burns to Fitzroy, which, if not attended to, the infection could kill him. A point Gus made to O'Neill as he watched on in dread.

"Two down one to go," Gus told O'Neill. O'Neill was quiet and visibly nervous.

"Keep it on six Alli and this time count to twelve!"

Freddie rolled Fitzroy out of position, turning away in shock, from the sight of the burn.

Freddie was at the back of O'Neill's head ready to roll him into position.

"Where is Emily O'Neill? Fitzroy can't answer me yet." Gus asked yet again, with a peal of laughter in his voice.

"Jesus Christ," Jake whispered to Jonty.

"I know." Jonty replied, as they both looked transfixed at Fitzroy's horrific injury.

O'Neill never answered. Freddie rolled him into position.

Alessandro had a dummy run, counting to twelve in front of O'Neill, this allowed O'Neill time to think whilst gauging how long the iron would be on his leg for. It seemed a long time.

For the third time, Alessandro cut the jeans from the waist to the knee, exposing O'Neill's leg. The steam was firing from the bottom of the plate. Alessandro pushed the water button to give it more effect.

Alessandro felt the iron in his hand like a glove, it felt warm, it felt comfortable, *a master at work*. he thought

Alessandro smiled into O'Neill's eyes and started to lower the iron.

"Stop, STOP! I will tell you!" O'Neill shrieked.

Alessandro did not appear to hear him at first, even though O'Neill couldn't have shouted any louder.

"Alli!" Gus shouted. Alessandro came to his senses and put the iron down.

Gus played it perfectly, he listened to Jonty and left O'Neill until the last, he knew O'Neill was the weakest, where a less experienced man may have put the leader, Fitzroy, last.

CHAPTER TWENTY-THREE.

MANCHESTER - NOVEMBER 1997

The now Archbishop Matthew Fitzpatrick was an elderly man, he lived and worked around Manchester for most of his life, he had encountered loyalist and republican violence. He had seen Manchester grow, sink and grow again. He had nothing but respect for the working community and how his Irish people contributed so much to the growth of the city, tracing back as far as the potato famine from, 1845 to 1849 where over one million Irish people died.

Thousands of Irish people made the emigration to the United Kingdom, many entering through the port of Liverpool and the veins spreading around, many into the city he had become to love, Manchester.

The archbishop had worked his way through life, beginning with the crime that saw him sentenced to prison. He moved his life forward through the Catholic Church first as a priest, then a bishop, with the last ten years as an Archbishop.

Now aged seventy-five Archbishop Matthew had lost his drive, he had lost his momentum but most of all he had lost his faith in people. He decided, finally to retire.

Age makes people reflect and Archbishop Matthew Fitzpatrick was no different. He felt guilt at the way he had progressed to his current position, all based on the dreadful tasks he completed for Roberto Sartori, and what for? A payment here a Payment there, leading to promotion through to his current position. He entered the church being a servant of God. He would leave it having been a servant of Roberto Sartori.

Matthew was feeling hypocritical, very hypocritical. Here he was an Irish man of the cloth. He lived in Manchester, a city he loved deeply, He was a servant of an Italian crime family, yet he did nothing to help the Irish people move forward.

The point that made the Archbishop decide his working life was to come to a halt, happened eighteen months earlier. A small number of his beloved Irish people damaged his beloved city.

He reflected on the Manchester bombing that changed his outlook on life forever.

***

MANCHESTER JUNE 15 1996

It was the IRA's biggest bomb containing 3,300 lbs of explosives, packed into a lorry left on Corporation Street in the heart of Manchester – it exploded just after 11.15 in the morning on Saturday the15th June 1996, the plan was to devastate the city, and shake the nation, it worked.

Archbishop Matthew thanked god that a warning was given to the police, who in turn managed to evacuate the streets of approximately 75,000 people. The explosion was so enormous it shattered windows in every building for several hundred yards. Two hundred people received injuries, some with only minor cuts, some with major lacerations. When Insurance loss adjustors instructed surveyors to inspect the city, they reported more than half a million square feet of retail space and at least another one hundred thousand square feet of office damage.

Manchester's jewel in the crown, The Arndale Centre, a massive tower building built in the early nineteen-seventies and clad in not so complimentary yellow tiles. Some Mancunians felt that the IRA had almost done the city a favour by hitting it, Archbishop Matthew could see their reasoning, Manchester had reinvented its self so many times over the centuries. He knew this could be a new opportunity to take the city into the new millennium, but he felt sad, sad that his Countrymen had hit a city that was raised and grew on the back of Irish love and labour.

Typical of the Manchester spirit, within hours of the explosion, the city's key players came together in a task force to deal with the pressing needs of more than six hundred businesses affected by the bombing, they were already planning to restore Manchester's now broken retail core. Two weeks later, the task force became Manchester Millennium Ltd, under the direction of Mr. Howard Bernstein, who took over as the city council's chief executive. He quickly persuaded business leaders the city could be successful again.

Fifteen minutes after arriving in Manchester, the Chairman of Marks and Spencer, Lord Seiff, announced it would completely rebuild its devastated premises to create the world's largest M&S, with three hundred and fifty thousand square feet of retail space. Other investors followed suit.

Archbishop Matthew was proud of his city and the tenacity it had always, and will always show.

The bomb caused three-hundred million pounds worth of damage, rebuilding the city centre would cost a total investment of £1 billion by the turn of the century.

Marks and Spencer went under construction along with a new street to link the upmarket shops around both St Ann's Church, a favourite of Archbishop Matthew, and Manchester's Cathedral. It will be the first pedestrian shopping street in Europe anchored by a church at one end and a cathedral at the other. This idea pleased Archbishop Matthew.

Manchester never loses a chance to promote itself, Matthew thought,

He also thought about the first Irish Lord Mayor elected in Manchester as long ago as 1923.

Mrs. Doherty was still Matthew's housekeeper, she had been with him since the early days of his priesthood at St Theresa's, they had laughed together, cried together and grieved together.

Mrs. Doherty always turned a blind eye to, Matthew's dealings with the Sartori family, which was important to Matthew.

Mrs. Doherty knocked on Matthew's door, breaking his thoughts.

"Mr. Sartori is here to see you, archbishop." Mrs. Doherty said, time never altered her respect in addressing Matthew correctly.

"Thank you, Mrs. Doherty, send him in please."

Giovanni walked in sombrely dressed, he wore an expensive designer made black tailored suit. With a pristine white shirt sat under it, with a black-tie. His black Italian leather shoes were highly polished, his black overcoat was draped over his arm, with black leather gloves held in one hand.

"Giovanni, how good to see you, let me take those off you." The archbishop took the overcoat and gloves off

Giovanni and placed them on a circular self-standing coat rack in the corner of the archbishop's study.

Usually, the pair would sit and discuss business around the archbishop's desk, which sat majestically in the room, with buttoned deep maroon leather seats either side of the solid mahogany desk.

Today Giovanni pointed to the three-piece chesterfield suite in the corner of the room,

"May we?" Giovanni gestured to the suite

"Of course," replied Matthew.

The suite matched the colour of the seats around Matthew's desk, with deep buttons and thick hide. The club chairs were very comfortable. Mrs. Doherty brought in a tray of tea and coffee, along with the usual piece of homemade fruitcake, for Giovanni's presence.

"How are you, Giovanni?" Matthew asked.

"I am well thank you archbishop" Giovanni was quieter than normal, a point that the archbishop did not miss.

"Archbishop, you have been a very good friend to Roberto and myself over the years, you have protected the family when asked, and you never questioned our motives."

"I have one last favour to ask of you archbishop."

"Anything Giovanni, you know that."

"I know now in your position, you no longer take the front line in ceremonies," Giovanni leaned and took a sip of the tea laid down by Mrs. Doherty.

"Archbishop, Roberto passed away this morning, and we are putting in place the final arrangements, the funeral is looking to take place in early December."

"Giovanni, please accept my commiserations and please pass them onto to Antonia and Francesca," Matthew answered.

"I would like you to take the funeral mass and burial archbishop, Roberto was a big character and we would like a big send-off."

"Of course Giovanni I would be delighted to take the proceedings."

Archbishop Matthew was silent for a few seconds,

"Giovanni, I also have a favour to ask?"

"Of course," Giovanni replied.

"None of us are getting younger, and I would like to retire from both the church duties and with your agreement, the family business."

"Granted Archbishop Matthew, I cannot think of a more fitting way to end a full and fruitful career than Roberto's funeral, You leave with my blessings," Giovanni replied.

You leave with my blessings. was further evidence of who Matthew was serving he thought.

"Thank you, Giovanni." Was all the archbishop could think of saying.

"I must be on my way, I have further things to organise, I will be in touch with the date in the next few days," Giovanni said.

"Thank you, Giovanni." The archbishop replied.

Mrs. Doherty smiled, as she pulled her ear away from the other side of the door, pleased that Matthew would no longer be involved with the Sartori family business.

CHAPTER TWENTY-FOUR.

December 13th, 1997

Fitzroy was still unconscious and did not hear O'Neill's shriek of an agreement to tell Jonty, Jake, and Gus where Emily was along with the added bonus of learning the whereabouts of Jones and Quinn.

"If you tell them, it will be the last thing you ever do!" Pitt shouted to O'Neill through gritted teeth still grimacing at the pain of the level two mark steam iron injury.

"Don't worry about him O'Neill," Gus said we have plans to keep you safe.

O'Neill looked at Gus with uncertainty, beads of sweat rolled down O'Neill's face.

"I will give you an example If you talk you will be kept alive, Mr. O'Neill." Gus continued.

Gus turned and looked at Freddie and Jim boy. "Fitzroy," Gus said.

"I will give you a hand," Alessandro said. It would help towards avenging his friend's killer.

Freddie and Jim Boy walked slowly to the bed Fitzroy was unconscious on, and wheeled it to the furnace at the bottom of the warehouse, opened the door and swung the body as they had earlier. "One, two, three!" They swung the body onto the hot coals, as they had with Luca before. Fitzroy never recovered from consciousness, the body lit with a high glow and then settled into a deep slow burn.

Jonty could not smell the body this time as he was far away, but the memory of the smell from Luca's burning body returned as if he was smelling it again.

Jake had been quiet through the proceedings he turned to Jonty "This can't be right, killing people and maiming them with the steam iron the way they did."

Jonty Replied. "I agree Jake but our priority is Emily, and without the death, Fitzroy could alarm people of her whereabouts."

"It's savagery," Jake whispered back.

"I agree," Jonty said and continued. "This is also our best shot at Jones and Quinn."

Jake nodded. He knew Jonty had considered all the alternatives.

Gus turned to O'Neill. "That's one less concern for you, Mr. O'Neill."

O'Neill looked at Pitt who had been a tough underworld man all his life, but he had never seen anything like this.

He looked at O'Neill and nodded, giving him the authority to tell Gus where Emily was. They both knew it was a life or death decision for them, they chose life.

"It's a shame we had to exert a little muscle to get to this stage, but here we are," Gus continued. "Where is Emily?" Gus looked directly into O'Neill's eyes.

"She is safe and well looked after, for the moment," O'Neill answered.

"But where is she?" Gus probed

"She is in a house in Norwalk." O'Neill spat out.

"Good, we are making progress," Gus responded. "Where in Norwalk?"

"It's off Main Street, about half a mile past Hickory Creek Cottage, It's called, Willow Barn. It's an old barn converted into a residential home." O'Neill answered.

"Anybody know Hickory Creek Cottage or Willow Barn?" Gus asked the room.

"I know it," Jake spoke out. "Hickory is a lodge out in the country off Main."

Gus turned to O'Neill. "Thank you, Mr. O'Neill."

Jake continued, "Norwalk is a city in Warren County. The city is part of the Des Moines West. Des Moines Metropolitan Statistical Area and is located just south of the Des Moines International Airport.

"OK, so we could be there in well under thirty minutes?" Gus asked.

"Yes," Jake replied.

Gus turned to Pitt. "You can choose which friend to join here Mr. Pitt, Mr. O'Neill or Mr. Fitzroy" Gus waited a few seconds for more impact. "Of Course Mr. Fitzroy was lucky, he died unconscious and unaware of what was happening, It will be different for you Mr. Pitt, you will enter the furnace alive."

Pitt stared back intensely, his face contorted with the pain of the burn and the fact that he had never 'talked' before, but he knew this was different, he knew Gus was not bluffing.

A decision had to be made, and now!

"What do you want to know?" Pitt finally asked, giving way to a chance of life.

"Tell me all about the security around Willow Barn?" Gus replied.

"What's in for O'Neill and me?" Pitt asked.

"I will guarantee your lives," Gus answered.

"How do I know you are not lying?" Pitt asked with a grimace as his burn pain shot up his leg.

"We are the Abano family, not a Paul Jones splinter group. We have built our reputation on our word," Gus went silent for a second, "For better or worse."

Pitt knew he had no choice, it was certain death or possible death, thinking about being thrown into the furnace alive turned his stomach at the core.

"Pitt answered the initial question. " Security is not watertight, the plan was to keep secrecy and attract no attention."

"Ok, and?" Gus answered, that comment made sense to him after all, they had only kidnapped a woman who would offer no threat of retaliation.

"The outside security is just the normal house alarm, not linked to the police for obvious reasons," Pitt added.

"Inside there are seven men, they stay at the house but work as two teams of three, on a shift system, covering her for twenty-four hours. Also, another is managing the situation and communicating with the woman's father for the money."

Gus asked. "So there are seven in total, to which three are sleeping in the day and four at night?"

"Yes, that's correct," Pitt answered.

"What artillery do they have?" Gus asked.

They have three handguns, which are kept in a box under the coffee table in the room where the woman is kept. A gun for each person on the working shift, if needed."

Thank you, Steve." Gus said, calling Pitt by his forename for the first time.

"That is one foot out of the furnace, let's keep the other one out," Gus said in his low, Barry White, drawl."

"Where are Billy Jones, ex-don, and John Quinn, ex-superintendent?" Gus asked.

"They are in England," Pitt replied.

Jonty looked at Jake. That was the last place they thought they would be.

"You wouldn't be playing me along on that would you?" Gus asked.

"They are in England," Pitt confirmed.

"What part of England?" Gus continued.

"Yorkshire," came, the reply.

Jonty looked at Pitt and took over from Gus. "What area in Yorkshire?"

"The Yorkshire Dales, they thought they could keep their heads low in the UK, as everybody would think they were outside of the Country."

"What part of the Yorkshire Dales?" Jonty pushed.

"I honestly don't know they wouldn't tell any of us. Not even Fitzroy."

"They tried a double bluff?" Jonty asked.

"If you like," Pitt replied.

"One final Question," Gus asked. "Do they have aliases?"

"Yes, Jones is using the name Robert Green," After Roberto and Billy's surname before his Mother remarried.

"And Quinn?" Gus asked.

"Colin Ashton."

Jonty turned to Jake, "England would have been the last place I would have looked."

"Same here," Jake replied.

"Thank you, Mr. Pitt, I forgot about your leg, it must be sore," Gus added.

"Luigi, Sort a meal out for Mr, Pitt and Mr. O'Neill, and get doctor Kirby, to look at Mr. Pitts's leg."

Kirby was a doctor used by the family. They paid him well for private family consultations.

Gus looked towards Jonty and Jake. "I need to talk to you both."

They walked into the annexe closing the door behind them and sat on the comfortable chairs and sofa. The log burner in the fireplace was doing its job in keeping it warm. Gus walked up to it, opened the door, before throwing two large logs through the door and into the burner.

Gus brought over three cups of hot coffee from the machine on the kitchen worktop. He placed it on the coffee table in front of them. He sat on the sofa and took up one and a half places. Jonty and Jake both sat in the adjacent armchairs.

"We are in a catch twenty-two here," Gus told Jonty and Jake. "How do we play it?"

Jonty and Jake stayed quiet they knew it was a rhetorical question.

"How do we approach this? If we find Emily and release her, word will soon get back to Jones and Quinn, and they will run for cover, knowing we gained the information from a close source. They will also be aware that Fitzroy, O'Neill, and Pitt are all unreachable because I am not releasing Pitt and O'Neill until this is all over. That, however, will send further warning signals." Jonty went thoughtful.

Gus continued, "If on the other hand we go for Jones and Quinn first, and that filters through to the team at Willow Barn, they may get nervous and harm Emily."

All were quiet, but all agreed.

Gus broke the silence after several minutes. "As I see it we have only one plan. We attack Willow Barn at night, as only three will be on guard and four sleeping, I suggest early hours."

That made sense to Jonty, as Gus continued, "Jonty, at the same time, you will attack the premises of Quinn and Jones, I am sure Giovanni Sartori will assist should you need it."

"We only know that Quinn and Jones are in the Yorkshire Dales, it's a big place," Jonty said.

"We know that Emily's father has been until the nineteenth of December to find the Money." Jonty nodded in agreement.

"I'll have Alessandro book the next flight back to the UK for you, you should be there tomorrow, that will be five days left and counting." Gus turned to Jake.

"Jake you can work from here with us. I know you would like to be around when we free Emily."

"If!" Jake said.

"When!" Gus reaffirmed.

CHAPTER TWENTY-FIVE.

December 14th, 1997.

Jonty landed in terminal one at Manchester Airport after his flight on American Airlines. Jet lagged and tired, he managed to steal a few minute's sleep but not quality sleep. A point not missed by Helen, as she met him at the arrivals gate.

"You look terrible." She said, "I hope you are not working for a day or two, you are not getting any younger."

"Unfortunately, I have to start work immediately; I have five days to ensure Em's release." He did not go into the detail of what he had seen over the last twenty-four hours, or that Billy Jones, who had been her Son's best friend, Paul, before giving the order to murder him in the hit and run twenty-three years earlier.

They drove home to their house in Eccles Manchester, where Jonty went for a shower, changed and ate the meal Helen had cooked him when he rang to say he would be landing in Manchester at eleven in the morning.

By two in the afternoon Jonty was in the offices and knocking on Superintendent Ron Morris' door.

Morris welcomed Jonty with, "Jonty I should sack you for leaving your position to fly halfway around the world on non-police business, give me a reason I should not?"

Jonty spent the next twenty minutes giving a selective summary to Morris of the events in Des Moines, omitting certain points such as bodies going into furnaces and steam irons torturing people for information.

"All I am asking sir, is that I am allowed to work on the case to bring in Jones and Quinn, Surely you want Quinn to be brought to justice too?" A point that Jonty knew was important to Morris.

"OK Jonty, but it must be done by the book, find out what part of Yorkshire they are in, notify the relevant police force, and keep it quiet in here. One thing I do know is this place has ears." Jonty agreed he had no idea who was on Billy's payroll.

"One final thing Jonty, You will have to do the background work alone as I have no extra hands to help you."

"I understand sir and thank you." Jonty was happy with that, the least people who knew the better the chance of success.

Jonty spent the afternoon trying to locate Jones and Quinn, or Robert Green and Colin Ashton as they were now known.

He sat at his computer screen and looked into records only police departments in the UK can access.

He went onto the obvious ones first, driving vehicle licensing, he typed in Colin Ashton, Yorkshire. Hundreds came up.

He then filtered it down to Yorkshire Dales postcodes. it filtered it down to around fifty.

He opened another screen and sat the two side by side. He did the same process for Robert Green. Many came up again.

His next plan was to look at both names on the separate screens to see if the two names came up with either one address of two very close by. No luck.

He followed the same process on tax records, television licenses, pensions, national insurance numbers, property deeds, council tax records, speeding fines, minor offences. Nothing showed under Robert Green or Colin Ashton with Yorkshire Dales postcodes living near to each other. Again without success.

He knew they would need a bank account, but under current law, he would need a court order which would take a day or two. This was the reason it was not his first route of inquiry.

He thought, he had no option, time was of the essence. Then a thought came into his head. *'Sir John Frasier.'* Jonty thought.

John Frasier was the chief executive of the National Bank. The bank used by Billy to launder money.

Jonty met with Sir John and discussed the accounts with Mike Chapman, the banks senior audit manager.

Jonty scanned his notes, from the meeting

Jonty thought back to meeting Sir John Frasier, informing him of the money laundering activated Paul Jones through his Company, Browns Engineering. Sir John invited Mike Chapman, the head of internal fraud, to the meeting to discuss the transactions.

Sir John sat in a large, wing-backed maroon leather chair with deep buttons. A large oak desk separated him from Jonty and Mike, who sat in chairs that were similar to Sir John's in colour and design, but of a smaller build.

Sir John looked very dignified in a navy suit with a grey broad pinstripe running down it. His tailored shirt was pure white and a crisp collar framed a navy tie with the National Bank's crest sitting proudly on it. Jonty estimated Sir John to be in his late sixties. He had a full head of grey hair and veins running down the bridge of his nose.

Wrinkles ran across his forehead, but his soft, aging skin showed no wrinkling down the cheek line.

   Mike Chapman was an expert on reading the internal systems and had the maximum authority of grade one. This allowed him to look through every part of any account. He opened the account of Browns Engineering online and talked it through with Sir John and Jonty. Jonty felt that huge strides were being made. He could feel the adrenalin flow through his veins, invigorating him.

   They spent the next forty-five minutes trying to understand the complex setup of the account. The first thing they noticed was an account balance of six million pounds, with a few markers from bank internal auditors to investigate periodically, with nothing ever followed up.

   Next to be noticed was a total of fourteen monthly standing orders made payable to another company, Greens Steel Ltd, each for the sum of £200,000. The Green Steel account, also held at the National Bank, showed numerous payments made to companies that included mainly well-known national steel and parts companies. Mike noticed Income was regularly returned, at an average of twenty percent lower than the outgoings.

   "This is a textbook way of taking dirty money and cleaning it," Mike told Sir John and Jonty.

   This account led to another account in the name of a restaurant, 'Verde Italia'. A detailed look at this account highlighted further anomalies. It had a regular monthly income from Brown's, but there were no outgoings normally expected from restaurant items such as food, utensils, cooking oils, alcohol, or wine.

   Mike looked further into the account, he noticed a BACS system paying a large number of individuals, with William Jones at the top of the list being paid £55,000 per month.

Jonty scanned down the list of recipients and noted another fifty names, with restaurant positions next to them, such as chef, waiter, cook, etc. Each payment made to an individual personal National Bank Account in the name of the recipients, which included Edward Le Conte, Jack Evans, Ken Fitzroy, James Pitt, and James Shepherd.

Jonty pointed out that Billy Jones was also employed by the bank as an area manager. He outlined that the reason for this was to allow him access and management from the frontline, thus allowing him to run the money laundering from the inside. He felt that there must be other 'employees' involved.

Mike took a sharp intake of breath and whistled.

"This is a classic layering exercise, without doubt," he stated.

"Why have internal audits not picked this up?" demanded Sir John in a very aggressive manner.

Mike's face flushed as he replied. "It has been picked up, Sir John. I will need to investigate why it hasn't been followed up."

"Nothing is more important in your life than getting to the bottom of this! Do you hear me?" Sir John's face was red with rage. He took it personally that somebody could take advantage of him through the bank.

"I hear you, Sir John," Mike answered. He felt a huge weight land on his shoulders, as well as some guilt that this was not spotted earlier.

He quickly did an internet search for Green's and the restaurant Verde Italia. They looked genuine from the search results. He rang the phone numbers advertised on the websites, but there was no reply from either. Instead, both numbers had the same answerphone message: "I am sorry but we are no longer in business to the public, we are sorry for any inconvenience."

Mike's next search was the Companies House register, which showed no sign of either business.

"They are illegal shell companies," said Mike. "They are used for nothing more than confusing transactions and cleaning up the laundered money by confusing the transaction trail."

Sitting in the three accounts was nineteen-million pounds being passed around like a game of pass the parcel.

Jonty looked through his contacts and came up with Sir Johns phone number.

The phone rang for the twentieth time that hour. Although you would not believe it the way Sarah Windsor answered the call.

"Good morning, Sarah Windsor, Sir John Frasier's secretary speaking."

The voice at the other end was straight and to the point.

"Good morning, my name is Detective Inspector Jonty Ball, is Sir John available, I must speak to him."

"I will see if he is available Detective Inspector," Sarah replied.

"Jonty, how are you?" the voice of Sir John boomed on the other end of the line.

"I am very well, thank you, Sir John," Jonty replied.

"Jonty, whenever you call it is usually not good news for the bank, tell me this is different."

"I am not sure, Sir John. I have further information about Billy Jones and I am trying to find out if he has an account with you?"

"Do you have a warrant Jonty?"

"No Sir John, it is a matter of urgency, I need it as a favour, I could get a warrant and get back to you in a day or two."

Sir John knew this could get into the wrong hands and initiate bad publicity.

"No Jonty, tell me what you want and I will look into it for you."

Thank you, Sir John, I am here until 6.00 pm this evening. Jonty looked down at his watch it was ten-past four.

Jonty gave Sir John the names of Robert Green and Colin Ashton and asked to look in the Yorkshire Dales within ten miles of each other.

"One last thing Sir John, the accounts have been opened in the last six months."

"I will do all I can Jonty." Sir John said.

"Thank you, Sir John," Jonty replied.

***

Des-Moines December 12th.

Halfway down Main Street, an old sign pointed to a right turn, the sign had faded burnt letters on it 'Willow Barn' The TV satellite van made the turn and drove down the road, which mainly consisted of stones and potholes.

It drew slowly to the gates of willow barn and stopped. Through a darkened window cut into the side panelling at the back, Luigi was busy taking photographs of the barn. The van proceeded a little further, stopped and Luigi took more photographs from a different angle, there was a sweeping turn that took the road around the side and then the back f the house. Luigi took more photographs.

Santi was driving, as he swung the van around to head bag with the photos, all taken, the sound of a helicopter was clear. Gus had organised overhead photographs, along with those taken from the van.

At the warehouse, Pitt and O'Neill were fed, Doctor Kirby was seeing to Pitt's steam iron burn, over the years he had learned not to ask, just to treat.

Pitt and O'Neill had showered and re-clothed in basic clothes, Pitt had an oversize pair of wrangler jeans, as did O'Neill, probably owned by the same large mobster. Pitt had a grey crew neck jumper with a matching colour fleece whilst O'Neill wore a navy polo neck jumper.

Both had cuffs around their ankles with a one-foot chain attached.

All was quiet when Gus turned to Jake and said. "I know Emily is your wife Jake, but it may be best if you stay away from the action, I can't afford to be looking after you. I don't want to carry passengers."

"Don't worry Gus I can look after myself I need to be there for Emily, whatever happens."

"OK Let's see if you can, you certainly have the muscle, but that doesn't mean you can fight," Gus said.

"I can. Don't worry about me, Gus."

Gus looked over at his men who sat laughing and joking now the first part of the job was complete.

He looked at Jim Boy, not an academic by any stretch of the imagination, but a great man to have around for muscle and heavy lifting.

Jim boy was 6foot 5 inches and weighing two hundred and fifty pounds.

"Jim boy, come over here a minute," Gus shouted over.

Jim Boy strolled over, he had jet black hair, crew cut style, he wore the dark blue boiler suit, he had yet to take off after his work around the furnace, a pair of black Nike training shoes with the familiar white tick on the side completed the look.

"Jim, Jake here wants to come with us when we find Emily, I need to know if he can look after himself."

Gus looked at Jake. "Are you prepared to fight Jim? It will prove if you may come along or not."

"Yes," said Jake. He rose knowing he would need to prove himself. Jim smiled.

"OK boss," Jim answered Gus.

Jake had a strong physic, he was tall, although a little shorter than Jim boy.

All the team stood round. To watch Jim prove Jake could not come along.

Pitt turned to O'Neill and whispered, "I'll have fifty-pounds on Hughes, do you fancy it?"

O Neill looked at Jim boy, then Jake and smiled, "deal." He told Pitt.

Pitt first encountered Jake eighteen months earlier. He and a couple of colleagues had received orders off Paul Jennings to, rough up, but not kill Jake. Paul felt Jake was getting a little too close on how the Sartori Family operated after a chance meeting in a Lake District Hotel.

He thought back to the day near Euston train station as Jake and Jonty travelled back from a regression meeting with an expert. Dr. Jameson, Jake was trying to convince a doubting Jonty that Jake was, Paul Jennings, the murdered man in a hit and run in Manchester in June 1977.

Pitt recalled Jake's fighting skills as he was walking to Euston train station with Jonty.

Pitt's orders were to rough up Jake and Jonty, but the opposite happened, He could see vividly in his mind's eye as he remembered boxing with Jonty whilst Jake was making mincemeat of his friend.

Jake looked over and could see Jonty was not getting the better of Pitt. Jonty's face was bloody and he was dragging a leg.

Jake hurled himself off the floor and a flying kick landed in Pitt's chest. Pitt man recoiled slightly. Jake instinctively widened his stance to give stability and, in the same movement, he threw a right hook towards the pitt's jaw. Pitt saw this early, he put up an arm and blocked it before he counterattacked, delivering a punch straight down the centre of Jake's bodyline and landing on his mouth. Jake felt the warm liquid smelter in his mouth. His lip cut.

Jake bounced forward on his left foot, delivering a perfect roundhouse kick to Pitt's jaw. In his anger, Pitt seemed to grow in stature, and he growled at Jake. This man knew how to fight. Jake stood bobbing up and down, keeping his body alert for any swift movement that may be needed. Jake threw another kick, hitting Pitt's solar plexus; the blow was hard, it was low and perfectly struck. Pitt reeled but did not go down. Jake could not believe it; nobody had ever withstood this kind of pressure from him, even at the American Nationals where he once fought.

Pitt straightened and grinned at Jake. "Is that all you have, son?"

It was designed to drain Jake's confidence. Although not drained, it was wilting. They squared up to each other again.

Flat cap shouted, "Jack, behind you!"

Too late, Jonty dropped the baseball bat over the Pitt's head like a woodsman felling a tree. Pitt fell to the ground, first to his knees. To help him on his way, Jake gave another roundhouse kick, just as Jonty delivered another baseball bat strike across the back of the neck.

I have yet to lose a fight, anywhere, but Hughes is the best I have faced, Pitt thought.

Pitt's memories of that day in Euston were shaken away by the sound of Jim's voice. It was a deep Bronx accent, obviously an American with an Italian background.

"Jake, you don't have to do this. I can't go easy on you as it will prove nothing." Jim Boy said in an apologetic voice.

"I know you can't Jim Boy, but I have to do it," Jake replied.

"Ok, let's get on with it," Jim answered.

Jim walked towards Jake, within seconds his face had changed from placid and tranquil into a contorted growling animal.

He made a swing for Jake with around fifty percent power, just to test Jake.

Jake ducked and it easily, the punch went over his head, Jake stood side-on to give him stability and to make himself a smaller target.

Jim came again, this time lower and straight down the centre, Jake simply took a step back and again Jim missed.

Jim now realised Jake may be agile enough to offer competition. The advantage Jim held was that he was fifty pounds heavier, the disadvantage, he was twenty years older than Jake.

Jim came to Jake again. This time he walked quickly to get close to Jake, not allowing him to move away as easy again, as he did Jake offered a right foot roundhouse kick that landed squarely on Jim Boys, ear, this was quickly followed up by a left-hand punch that added extra force as Jim walked onto it from the previous blow.

Jake made half a turn and lowered his head, making his torso parallel with the floor, and delivered a kick with the sole of his foot in Jim Boys midriff, Jim let out a groan.

"Enough," Gus shouted. "I don't need any injured men, it will be tough enough as it is."

Gus turned to Jake, smiled, and said. "You're in."

***

As the clock hit five pm exactly, Jonty's telephone rang.

"Jonty Ball." He answered, spilling some coffee onto his desk as he moved enthusiastically to pick up the phone.

It was the call he wanted but was the information he wanted about to be revealed.

"Jonty, John Frasier here."

"Hello Sir John, thank you for getting back before the end of the day."

"Jonty I have the information you require. Both Robert Green and Colin Ashton have opened accounts in the last six months, with addresses in the North Yorkshire area."

Jonty could feel the energy injecting into what had been a tired body all day.

"They are both registered in Richmond, North Yorkshire. Green lives at Waterfall House and Ashton at Ripon Rise. Both houses are on Reeth Road."

"Thank you very much, Sir John, I will get to work on it first thing in the morning."

"Jonty I want no bad publicity from this, if it is further money laundering, I want it quelling and quelling discretely, do you understand?"

"I do understand?" Jonty replied, "You have my guarantee."

"One last thing before I go." Sir John said to Jonty.

"Yes Sir John," Jonty asked.

"Both accounts have more than one million pounds in them!"

The phone went dead.

Jonty decided to call it a day, he said good evening to the staff and made his way home to the terraced house he shared with Helen, in Sadler Street, Eccles.

On his arrival, Helen had cooked a hearty meal of steak, fries, and onions, one of Jonty's favourites.

Over tea, Helen asked many questions, particularly about the safety of Emily. Helen and Em had grown particularly close when she was in England with Jake.

CHAPTER TWENTY-SIX.

Helen's story

Helen lost a son, Paul, twenty-five years earlier in a hit and run incident after a night out with his, then best friend Billy Jones.

Unbeknown to Paul, Billy was living a life in his grandfather's crime business.

His grandfather was Roberto Sartori. Roberto had built several businesses over his long life ranging from, running speakeasies in the New York prohibition era, high earning protection rackets in the mining industry, protecting mine owners from workforce strikes. He masterminded this by paying money to union leaders, who in return, ensured no strikes happened. He paid them from the income he received from pit owners, before nationalisation when it became the National Coal Board on January first. 1947. He kept the remainder for himself, which was a very healthy income.

Towards the end of World War II Roberto bought an engineering company, forced by the government to stop the production of luxury motor parts, to producing munitions for the war effort. He planned initially, continue making arms for the good of the country in its efforts in the war.

Following the war, he continued the company continued manufacturing, rifles, shotguns, and handguns, to a high standard. He sold some of it legally, to make the company look legitimate, He then sold the majority on the black-market, to any conflict in the world, uprisings, civil wars, country conflicts etcetera. He had no allegiance to any side and often sold his stock to both sides in the same conflict.

Billy was responsible for the export of the stock, deporting them from Liverpool Docks. He regularly talked people into transporting them to the docks and paid them, large sums of money for doing it.

Billy, however, could not allow the operation to be leaked. The risk was too high, with that in mind he regularly ordered the demise of people after a few deliveries.

One person coerced into a delivery was Paul Jennings, Helen's son, Billy tricked Paul into running two cargos' for export and decided to end the association, particularly as Paul told Billy he did not want to do the gun-running any longer. Billy was shocked that Paul knew what the deliveries were, as he had always kept the contents a secret from the drivers.

Billy and Paul, Billy also used his then fiancé and future wife, Maggie, into a game where they would meet up in a bar pretending not to know each other, a game Maggie liked the idea of. Billy liked the idea of an alibi if needed.

Maggie looked forward to the evening in Manchester. She was celebrating her friend, Jane's, twenty-first birthday. Billy thought it could tie in nicely with his plan. A job he knew he needed to do.

"Let's play out a fantasy I have," Billy said to Maggie.

"Oh, yes? And what would that be?" she answered with a knowing smile.

"When you go to Manchester, let's meet up in a pub and pretend we don't know each other," he replied.

"And?" Maggie giggled.

"I will come over and chat you up before we come home together," said Billy.

Maggie giggled again. "Oooh, I like that idea! Let's do it," she teased. Billy knew that Paul had not met Maggie – or, indeed, knew of her. He also knew it was a perfect alibi.

The night of the party was passing on. By ten o'clock, the pints turned quickly to Jack Daniels and cokes to ease the pressure on the already bursting stomachs swilled with pints of Boddington's and Holts' bitter, the local Manchester ales.

As usual, Billy was popular with the girls, he was showing a particular interest in a bubbly blonde doing a bad rendition of Candy Staton's 'Young Hearts Run Free' on the pub karaoke. However, the short skirt and big smile seemed to make up for that in Billy's book.

"I think I am going on to a club with young Candy," joked Billy to Paul later in the evening.

"No problem," replied Paul. "I should be getting home to make sure Sue is okay." Sue was Paul's pregnant wife.

Paul finished his drink before continuing. "Catch up on Monday. Keep me up to date with Candy, sharing her one and only life!" he added, referring to a line in the song. They laughed and shook hands, Paul left and walked into the city night.

Five minutes after Paul left, Billy turned to Maggie to tell her he was going to the toilet. She smiled and returned to the girls celebrating the twenty-first – who, like Paul, had no idea Billy and Maggie were a couple.

Billy walked out of the main part of the crowded pub and towards the gents. He made a quick right into a red telephone box the pub had bought for authenticity. He searched his back pocket and brought out a neatly folded piece of A4 paper. He unfolded it to reveal a mobile telephone number. Billy dialled the number and Steve Pitt answered.

"He has just left!" Billy said down the phone.

"I'm on my way," Pitt replied.

"Do you have the black BMW parked around the corner with the new plates on it?" Billy asked,

"Yes."

"Perfect!" Billy answered. "Good luck."

"Luck doesn't come into it," Pitt said, the line went dead.

Billy walked back into the bar area and headed towards Maggie. "What did you say your name was again?"

"I didn't," she replied with a wink.

***

JUNE 1977, MANCHESTER, ENGLAND

The car eased through the automatic gears as it proceeded into the drizzly Manchester night. It was no different from the hundreds of times the driver had done this before; a night on the town, a few more drinks than normal, the mood throughout had been free and easy. It began at seven in the evening with a few drinks shared with four friends, which increased to eight by ten-thirty. It seemed that all the usual crowd had the same idea on that warm, sultry night, until the yellow, closing sun gave way to the first dark clouds, and then the rain. The city centre was quietening down as the midnight news on the radio was followed by the dulcet tones of Bryan Ferry singing the Dobie Gray classic, 'The In Crowd'. It all seemed to match the mood of the night.

A taxi ride of only a few miles seemed pointless compared to the disruption of returning on public transport in the morning, only to drive back home in the Saturday hustle and bustle of the shopping fraternity.

As the car floated around the corner of Portland Street and into Peter Street, an unwelcome vision appeared in the rearview mirror. The police patrol car was looking for any disruption in the city streets.

In a moment of panic, the police car woke up the street with flashing blue lights and unfriendly sirens.

Here we go! thought the driver. However, as quickly as the thought came into his mind, the orange and white car flashed past the BMW, racing towards a more pressing problem elsewhere. *It must be my lucky night*! A feeling of invincibility radiated. The driver relaxed into the seat and slid the radio button to the off position.

Within a minute, a body hit the car with a dull, sickening thud, followed by a head hitting the windscreen! The pedestrian was instantly recognised. Paul Jennings! They knew each other, sometimes drank together, always chatted and shared a laugh when they met. This was different. Paul Jennings had been struck by the car and, as if in slow motion, Jennings rolled up the bonnet and onto the windscreen. Their eyes met and, in what must have been a split second and felt like five minutes, they instantly recognised each other, before the strength of bone outmatched the strength of glass and the crack in the windscreen appeared like a sheet of ice forming on a freezing pond.

The body lay, contorted, on the wet kerb. Nobody was around, the rain must have kept people off the streets. What decision must the driver make? Was he dead?

The car drove out of the city with a bruised bonnet, a cracked windscreen, a driver high on alcohol, whilst a stiff, motionless body lay strewn in the street.

Within, three weeks Paul was buried on, a hot sweltering Manchester day, leaving behind his pregnant wife, Sue, and his devoted mother, Helen.

Helen stood by the grave, her mind elsewhere. Within days, she had met the detective given the responsibility of finding her son's killer. Jonty Ball was a tough-looking man in his late thirties to early forties, with cauliflower ears from years of semi-professional boxing. He stood six foot six inches and weighed in at nineteen stone. He loved nothing more than getting involved in a fight with Manchester's finest. He was the top dog and everyone knew it.

He had asked the routine questions. "Where had Paul been going?" "Why was he going?" "What was he doing there?" Stupid questions asked, all irrelevant. The lads had been going for a pint on a Friday night in the City. He was determined to find an end to this, despite Helen's response.

"Hang on a minute here," Helen had said. "My son is the victim, not the aggressor. Please treat this case as such!"

"I know," Jonty said. "I will do all I can to find the person responsible and give you closure."

Helen still had the body of a young woman, it belied her age of 38. She was still an attractive woman, although, the long blonde locks of yesteryear now replaced by yellow hair from a bottle in an attempt to disguise the grey.

Helen and Jonty had a synergy that kept them friends and eventually man and wife.

They met again under a strange circumstance. Helen was at home one day when there was a knock on the door.

"Are you Mrs. Jennings?" Jake asked.

"Yes," the woman replied.

"Mrs. Helen Jennings?"

"Yes!"

"Could we speak to you in private?"

"Not really," the woman replied. "When Americans come here, they are usually Jehovah's Witnesses or something!"

"I am not a Jehovah's Witness, or a salesman or anything," said Jake. "I just want to chat."

Helen looked at Jake and thought how handsome he looked. He had a very good physique that was emphasised by the navy blue tight-fitting Fred Perry tee-shirt and a pair of cream chinos with brown, well-polished, Oxford shoes. Em was equally as smart, in a black and white polka dot ankle-length skirt and a white shirt with black braiding on the top pocket and black buttons.

"No, not today, thank you," said Helen.

As the door closed in Jake and Em's faces, Em shouted out spontaneously.

"It's about Paul!" There was no response. "Paul. Your son Paul!" The second comment was as loud as she could muster.

The door reopened. Helen looked at them blankly. "You better come in then."

Jake and Em glanced at each other and followed Helen into the hallway and then into the lounge. Em quickly felt comfortable in the room with its high, pristine white ceilings and pastel green walls. There was a log burner set in what would have once been an old fireplace, with the original stone surrounding it in the hearth. They were invited to sit on an antique green leather couch, which was deep and wide.

"Well, what do you want to talk to me about?" said Helen. "Please make this quick as I have to be out in ten minutes."

Silence echoed around the room for a good thirty seconds until a grimace fell on Helen's face. "Tell me now!"

Jake cleared his throat. "As you can tell, I am from America, Iowa." His mid-west accent drew out the Iowa in it. He continued. "My name is Jake Hughes and this is my wife, Em… I mean Emily. I have never been to Manchester before, but I know my way around it like I have been living here all my life!."

"That's right!" said Em. "I couldn't believe it!"

Helen intervened. "I am pleased for you. Is that what you came to tell me?"

"No." responded Jake. "I have come to tell you I know who killed Paul." The room fell silent. The room felt heavy. The room felt thick and airless.

Helen stared. "So, you, an American, who has never been to Manchester, claim to know how my son died after the best of the English police force couldn't find out. Please leave my house!"

"Give me fifteen minutes," Jake pleaded. "I need to tell you a story you will not believe. I am not even sure Em and I do, but please hear me out."

Helen looked at him for a moment. *What is this nutcase going on about?* she wondered. Then a second thought. *Oh well, there is nothing to lose!*

"You have ten minutes, then you need to leave!"

"Thank you!" said Em.

Jake cleared his throat. "I am finding this difficult to say, as you have lost a son and I don't want to rekindle any sad memories. You will either take my opening line with an open mind or you will think I need psychiatric help."

"What is your opening line?" Helen enquired.

"I am Paul reincarnated!"

Helen stared at Jake. "I will take the psychiatric choice. Get out now!"

"But…"

"Out! Now!" Helen's face was red with thunder as she stormed to the door.

Jake began to panic. "You loved northern soul music, you went to a club in Manchester called the Twisted Wheel," he said quickly. "My favourite food was egg as a kid. I fell and bent my front teeth aged about five. I had ten stitches in my calf when I was seven!"

Helen looked at him. "Are you stalking me? Have you been doing research just to upset me?"

"You once cooked a bag of fish in butter sauce in boiling water, and burst the bag because it said pop bag in boiling water, then you realised it didn't mean burst the bag in boiling water. You told me never to mention it to anybody!" Jake was grabbing at straws now.

Helen put her hand up to her mouth. "How do you know that?"

"I don't know," said Jake. "I didn't even know I did until thirty seconds ago!"

"You are weird," said Helen. "You can't know all this!"

"I remember my father's registration on a Hillman car. BVB 378J! You smoked Park Drive cigarettes and liked iced lollies with a brand name Mivvi, and I don't know where any of this is coming from!" Jake was shouting now. He was like a man possessed. Em had never seen him like this before.

"Ok!" said Helen "You have all the facts. Let me ask you some questions. How much did you give me out your first weekly wage?"

"Fifteen pounds!" was the reply.

"What was the name of your toy teddy bear?"

"Scruff. It was passed down from my cousin Jane!"
"What date did you die?"
"I don't know."
"Well, if you don't know the basics of when you died, how can you be reincarnated?" Helen countered. "What is your date of birth?"

"The fifteenth of March 1985," Jake replied, but with less certainty.

"You have hit some personal points and I don't know how you came across them," said Helen. "But how can I believe you are my son reincarnated? How? You don't even know his birthday." She waved her hands in confusion. "I have to go now, so please leave!"

"Well, that's the end of the story, morning glory," said Em as they finally hit the M62 heading west towards Preston. They were sitting quietly, thinking what might have been, when they both jumped. Jake's phone was ringing. Em answered as there was no hands-free in the car.

"Wow! Gosh! Really," Em said into the phone. "Why didn't we think of that? Ok, we are on our way now."

"Who was that?" Jake asked.

"It was Helen!" said Em excitedly. "She said she'd been thinking about your date of birth."

"And?"

"She said that Paul died on June fifteen, 1984!"

"And?" Jake asked again.

"Well, you were born exactly nine months after Paul died, the time your mom was carrying you."

Jake looked at Em. It was all fitting into place again.

"She wants to see us now!" Em's voice raised to an excited shrill.

"Sadler Street, here we come!" Jake replied with equal enthusiasm.

From that point, the world changed for them all as each step drew nearer to the guilt of Billy Jones.

As Jonty dug deeper into the case he found that there were many police officers on the payroll of Billy, including his ex-partner and close friend Jimmy 'Shep' Shepherd and his reporting officer, Superintendent John Quinn.

Quinn had masterminded the plot to free Billy from a hostage situation at his own home. This was successful and the two remained on the run.

Over the Months, Jonty, Jake, Emily, and Helen became very close. Helen was very concerned after the discovery of Em's kidnapping. She had grown fond of her like a daughter, along with Jake as the son he had proved to be, even if it was through his reincarnation.

CHAPTER TWENTY-SEVEN.

December 15th –Manchester

Jonty sat at his desk by eight in the morning, the office was desolate except for a few night staff finishing paperwork ready to swap their shifts in an hour or so.

He was due to meet Superintendent Morris at nine-thirty and wanted to utilise the time beforehand planning his trip to Richmond, Yorkshire.

By the time nine-thirty arrived, Jonty had booked an appointment with Roger Miller, the North Yorkshire Superintendent, for nine the following morning, at Alverton Court, the North Yorkshire Police Headquarters, he tried for that afternoon but Miller could not, or would not oblige, Jonty left the conversation unsure of which. He booked a hotel in Richmond, The Frenchgate, named after the road it sat on, booked a car from the carpool available from one pm later that day, he finally looked on a property website to see when Ripon House and Waterfall House both sold.

The properties were bought within a week of each other back in June of that year. Both properties were also bought at the asking price, unusual, as most purchasers negotiate a price downwards.

Jonty knocked on Morris's door at nine-thirty prompt.
"Come in."

Jonty walked through the door. The office had changed since the days of Quinn, but only marginally, Quinn's pictures had disappeared to replaced by Morris's family photos, along with a signed photo of Denis Law, Morris's favourite footballer from many years ago. He was an ardent Manchester United fan and, whom Law played for.

The desk was a large light oak with a large winged chair in matching wood along with a fabric-padded seat in navy blue, to add comfort. The chair opposite matched the wood but had lower back support and arms sat at the same height, making it a club chair. Jonty sat in this chair.

"Jonty where are you up to with the investigation?" Morris asked.

Jonty told Morris about the addresses, and when they were bought.

"Does it link in with the kidnapping in Des-Moines?" Morris continued.

"I have no further dealings with the Des-Moines incident, sir," Jonty lied, "It is up the United States people to deal with that now." Jonty purposefully did not use the word authorities and used the word people which meant technically he was not telling lies, although he was condoning criminals taking affairs into their own hands.

"Very wise Jonty," Morris said with a nod.

So all you have to be concerned with is bringing Jones and our ex-colleague Quinn to trial?"

"Yes, sir that's about the brunt of it."

"Superintendent Miller, do you know him?" Morris asked.

"No Sir."

"Typical Yorkshireman, blunt and to the point, but a good man, I am sure he will help all he can." Morris continued. "Is that all Jonty?"

"No sir, I was wondering about manpower, can I request support?" Jonty asked.

"Not at this stage, Miller may be able to assist, but I have no slack, we are undermanned for our day to day work, Government cuts, you know what it is like Jonty."

"I understand sir," Jonty replied, not understanding a government hell-bent on reducing police on the street whilst inviting an increase in crime rate.

Jonty picked up the car, a white, Volvo V70XC. Jonty requested this model because it is as reliable and as safe as any Volvo on the road, it has comfort for long trips and most of all. The four-wheel-drive XC model is a huge plus in the winter months as the car is completely stable in snow or on slippery roads. This would probably be required in December in the Yorkshire Dales.

It was one-thirty by the time he signed for the car, loaded his suitcase and ensured the tank was full of petrol. He had dressed casually for the day as he knew he had a three-hour drive ahead of him, he had several routes available but chose the M6, even though longer in miles, experience told him there would be no traffic congestion.

He drove from Manchester and connected with the M6. He drove north for around an hour before exiting at junction 36, by now the city buildings had turned to the Lake District fells and countryside. He turned right and pointed the Volvo towards Kirkby Lonsdale, within fifteen minutes left Kirkby Lonsdale behind and was quickly into the Yorkshire Dales, he never realised how close the two national parks were to each other until today, however he still had a two-hour drive ahead of him. After a further few miles, the satellite navigation system took him left signposted, Ingleton. He followed this road for about another mile and the countryside hit him like a sledgehammer in the face. Stunning open fields, with grass kept under control by sheep, thousands of sheep! He tracked a gentle creek meandering around the vast wilderness. The green turned white where the snow from previous days had settled.

He drove on for another thirty minutes passing only a handful of houses, Farms, and many barns used to store food for the sheep in the winter months. He quickly dropped into Hawes. He knew he was halfway through his journey, he stopped for a coffee at the Wensleydale Cheese Factory, famous for its stunning cheese, sold worldwide. The public could visit the factory and see the cheese produced, to add to the commerciality they had added a café and a restaurant.

He finished his coffee and continued towards Leyburn, passing through Askrigg famous for the popular television programme, all creatures great and small. He finally reached Leyburn and pushed on, it was now snowing heavily as he ventured further north. The scenery was stunning. He finally entered Richmond. He turned off Pottergate, into Frenchgate, and rested the car's engine in the hotel car park. It was five ten Pm and hopefully one hundred and fifteen miles nearer to Quinn and Jones.

***

Ten days passed since Christopher Connaught first received the call from the man with the East European accent, he had lost half a stone in weight through worry and sickness, his wife Rachael was having panic attacks. She pleaded with Christopher to re-contact the police. "I won't do that." he told her, "They are too slow and they were not interested when we first contacted them." He said.

It was twelve after noon, Christopher's phone rang "Hello!" he snarled down the phone, the lack of sleep had made him angry, his daughter had been kidnapped, that made him angry, he was being blackmailed with no police support, that made him angry.

"It is now the thirteenth of December Christopher." The east European voice was unmistakable. "I thought I would call you and check on your progress."

"I have until the nineteenth, don't you dare put any more pressure on me!" he snarled down the phone.

"No pressure here Christopher, I am just calling to say that from the twentieth you will be getting your daughter back." The European voice told Christopher.

In the second's Christopher felt relief,

"Piece by piece." The voice said next.

Stress returned to Christopher.

Christopher slammed the phone down, picked up the receiver again, then pushed the buttons.

"Good afternoon, Jonty Ball speaking." Jonty had entered his hotel room two minutes earlier.

"Jonty, Christopher again, how is the search for Emily going?"

"We are not as far on as we would have liked Christopher." Jonty lied in case Christopher's phone was tapped.

"What do you intend to do next Jonty?"

"I am back in the UK Christopher, trying to solve another case."

"I have funded all this money for what?" retorted Christopher, for you to gallivant in America and return to the UK?" He slammed the phone down.

Jonty felt guilty but secrecy was the most important part at this stage, just in case.

Jonty quickly showered and decided to phone Helen to let her know he had arrived safely before a meal and an early night in bed.

After chatting to Helen about his journey and an update on how bad he felt following the discussion with Christopher he decided to have a drink before his evening meal in the bar.

He sat in a comfortable room just off the bar, the room was long with a high ceiling painted cream, it had an ornate chandelier falling from the ceiling. There were two windows sat at ninety degrees to each other, one a sash window, with three sets of cream curtains, one on each side of the window, the other in the middle, all were draped. The other adjacent window boasted sixteen smaller squared windows inset, each with wooden beading, and two matching drapes at each end of the window. Two cream suites stretched down the length of the wall, different in style but both dressed in fabric, with matching cream and maroon vertical stripes. A large, lit, log burner set in the opposite wall, in front of the log burner sat two matching brown leather chairs with deep buttons, between them sat a high wooden coffee table made in mahogany with a glass top. Jonty settled in one of these chairs. Jonty sat in the room alone, he ordered a Jack Daniels and coke with ice. He sat back and rested for the first time in several days.

***

Des-Moines December 13th

Gus and the team sat the team in a conference room at the Newark Liberty International airport hotel, the same room Paul Conchetti had delivered his speech along with Gus three days ago.

Gus loaded a DVD linked to the large TV screen mounted upon a wall.

Gus fired up the screen the first photograph showing the front of the Willow Barn. They were the photographs taken by Luigi and Santi.

"This is the front of the barn, nothing out of the ordinary," there said Gus.

He followed with all six pictures taken from the van and nothing, on the outside at least worried them, it was alarmed yes, but just a normal security alarm.

One picture was of the alarm box, which Luigi had zoomed in on.

"Luigi, tell us a little about the alarm system." Gus smiled at him.

Luigi rose to his feet. "The system is a home protection system by a company called the Peace of Mind Alarm Company." He showed another picture, this time it was of the system he took from the Peace of Mind Website.

Luigi continued, the system has a lot of what we would expect from the basics of an alarm system, you will all remember when all we wanted from a system was a system that beeped when you opened the door, then triggered the alarm. Maybe you had magnetic sensors, too much wiring hidden anywhere from around skirting boards being buried in your walls, a strange-looking control panel that offered only cryptic codes and signals down the phone lines when an emergency occurred." Everybody in the room smiled and nodded at this

Luigi continued, "Home security features will always need the basics. Sensors, door chimes, and the heart of any home security system is still a control panel that can be connected to a remote alarm monitoring service." Luigi took the presentation to the next page. This system is modern, but nothing to be fearful of, the main difference is it is now Wireless Technology." Luigi said trying to make it sound as simple as he could.

"Think of it as the same as the smartphones you have in your pockets or tablets that allow us to be free from desk-bound PCs. It is just the same. This advancement also makes way for camera, technology, which allows us to see people in full High Definition colour. There are two external cameras on the building." Luigi showed pictures of the two cameras, one around the back and one on the corner at the front right-hand side of the house.

"Now my guess is they will not have alarms bells, because that will attract unwanted attention, after all, they have a hostage in there, why would they want to attract the feds. They may have smoke alarms and we need to think they have, as a contingency."

"Thank you, Luigi," Gus said, Luigi nodded and sat down.

"We also took photographs from above." Gus continued, whilst advancing the presentation.

"Here is an overhead view of Willow Barn. It's the footprint." Gus continued.

The barn was in the shape of an 'L' at the front portion was a large double garage, at the end of that was the accommodation. It was built over two stories.

"Santi has looked at the initial plans online, when the planning permission was accepted, there are six bedrooms and two reception rooms," Gus continued.

"We have three problems as I see it.

One. How do we get into the property?

Two. Is Emily actually in the property?

Three. If she is how do we know which room she is in?" time will be of the essence.

Gus let these comments hang before continuing.

"We need to think that through, however, time is our enemy, any ideas are welcome. We have only a few days before the ransom is expected to be paid." Gus said as he let the meeting end there.

CHAPTER TWENTY-EIGHT.

December 16th Richmond.

Jonty turned up for his meeting with Superintendent Roger Miller ten minutes earlier than the agreed time. For the first time in over a week, he donned a working suit, more appropriate to his job. He wore a navy two-piece suit fresh from the dry cleaners, which looked sharp, a first time worn crisp white shirt. A bold red tie to add colour held down by a solid silver tiepin that gripped the tie to the shirt, the tiepin given to him on his return from America by Helen, as an early Christmas present. The outfit was finished off with shiny black leather shoes and a black belt with a silver buckle, which matched the tiepin.

Miller turned up ten minutes late, a trait Jonty had always hated, he felt it showed disrespect to others.

"DI Ball, take a seat please, have you been offered a drink?" Miller asked.

"I have. Thank you, sir." Jonty replied hiding his disgust at there being no apology for Miller's lateness.

Miller spoke in a broad Yorkshire accent as he moved a large pile of unorderly paperwork from his desk to the floor. "I am not up to speed with your reason for being here, can you update me?"

Jonty took a second to take in the fifty-something man, sat opposite him.

Miller had a full head of unkempt grey hair that was longer than would be expected for a man in his position, it was over his collar at the back and his ears at the side, it looked like it also had not seen a comb that morning.

His shirt was white, but after many years had the yellow cast that often comes with cheap white shirts after a while. The uniform whilst neat was not what Jonty would call pristine. Jonty's last sight was of a stomach hanging over his trousers, which looked firm and visceral.

Jonty replied, "Sir I have reason to believe that two suspected fugitives are on the run in your area."

"Tell me more?" Miller asked.

Jonty picked up the story. "The two suspects are ex-superintendent John Quinn and Billy Jones, the leader of a crime family. Eighteen months ago Jones was surrounded by specialist police marks-men. Jones was the main suspect for Murder, gun running, money laundering, tax evasion, and many more crimes."

Jonty took a sip of his now cold coffee before continuing. "Quinn devised a plan, to assist Jones in an escape using his position, as superintendent, as the decoy. They both escaped in a private jet."

"I am aware of the Quinn situation, Ball" Miller interrupted, "Carry on without too much detail."

Jonty continued,"Earlier this month a young woman, Emily Hughes, the wife of Jake Hughes, a man integral to helping identify Quinn and Jones from the outset, was kidnapped, in Des-Moines, Ohio."

"Do you know the reason for the kidnap, and how does it link in?" Miller asked.

"We believe the reason followed a closing down of their money laundering accounts, in the name of Browns Engineering Company, Jones was the Managing director," Jonty added.

"Sir John Frasier, the chief executive of the National Bank, helped no end in closing the accounts down, of which there were multi-millions of pounds."

"Where does this link in with the kidnapping?" Miller continued.

"Emily Hughes,s' Father is a rich man, Christopher Connaught," Jonty added, "He has been asked to pay a ransom of two million pounds by December the nineteenth, this Friday. We believe this is to cover a debt owed, by Jones, to a South American drug baron, a business associate. He could not pay due to his assets being frozen by the National Bank."

"So where do I fit into all this?" Miller asked.

"Investigations tell us that, despite us believing Quinn and Jones lived abroad, they actually live in England, Richmond specifically," Jonty answered. "They are living under false names, Quinn, Colin Ashton, and Jones, Robert Green."

"I am here for two reasons sir." Jonty said, "One, to show my respect by telling you what is happening on your patch."

"And two?" Asked Miller.

"Two, sir is that I need support from your district. I plan to enter the properties around 8.00 am," Jonty said. He was not specific why eight, but he knew it coincided with 3.00 am local time in Des-Moines after Gus had requested a simultaneous attack, he wanted to attack in the early hours, knowing four of the kidnappers would be asleep and three guarding Emily, this would give maximum efficiency for Gus.

"When do you want the operation to Happen DI Ball?"

"Friday the 19th sir," Jonty responded.

"That's three days away, we would need to find a team capable, debrief them, train them and the little factor of a search warrant," Miller replied.

"Quinn, also, will be very familiar with the law. He will know his rights to privacy under Article 8 of the Human Rights Act, which could be used to argue against an unlawful arrest." Jonty had not thought of this, but equally, he knew Quinn was guilty, but knowing and proving are two, totally, different things.

"We will need to write to the Magistrates court for permission, and, IF!" Miller raised his voice to say if. "IF! the court grants the warrant, we would not have the time to execute, because I would not want to put a plan in place until the plan is authorised, if it was declined I would be wasting time on resources and money," Miller added.

"We can have a court order by the end of the day." Jonty contested.

"Then two days to de-brief a team and have them ready for a Friday attack, THIS WEEK! It's impossible, all too rushed DI Ball, I would be prepared to do it say, mid-January?" Miller added.

"It needs to be Friday, sir, we will miss the opportunity if not," Jonty argued.

"The answer is NO! DI Ball, it is not enough notice." Miller emphasised the no.

Jonty gave a hard stare to Miller.

"Is there anything else DI Ball? I have a busy day ahead of me."

"No sir, thank you for your time," Jonty replied and walked out of the office.

Jonty went back to his hotel and drank a coffee in front of the fire on the same chair as the evening before to think things through.

Jonty searched his pocket for his mobile phone. He only had one option. He punched in the numbers.

The phone rang out and answered at the other end.

"Giovanni, I know you are still recovering, but I must see you, I am in Richmond Yorkshire." He glanced down at his watch it read ten-fifteen. "Can I come over to Cheshire this afternoon to meet with you about a plan I have, regarding the matter we have been involved in lately?" He was sure not to be too specific.

"Of course Jonty, what time were you thinking of?" Giovanni replied.

Around two this afternoon, is your house Ok?"

"Yes see you then Jonty," Giovanni replied.

He still doesn't make chatting on the phone for a long experience. Jonty thought as he went back to his room to collect his car keys.

***

December 16th Des-Moines. Ohio.

Gus thought until his brain ached about how he could identify which room Emily was held in, he asked Luigi, and Alessandro, they could not think of a way without strong using arm tactics, which was the last thing Gus wanted to do whilst Emily was held hostage.

Jake approached Gus, "Gus I have an idea."

Gus turned to Jake and asked what it was.

"If we get Pitt to call the kidnappers to say that they are worried about the alarm system, and he has asked an engineer to check it just in case it's needed."

Gus looked at Jake and saw some mileage in it. "If I send Luigi, he would be able to look at the system and check around," Gus added.

He called Luigi over. "Luigi if we could get into the house under the pretence of you being an engineer, what could you do?"

"I could look at the system, Emily obviously would be placed out of sight, somewhere safe but I could look for clues, maybe."

"And what about a van with the Company name on the side, is anyone on the payroll from the company?" Gus asked.

"Not that I am aware of." Luigi replied, "But we have a Company on the payroll who makes signs for any occasion, they could make a sign for the van."

"Great, Go on the internet and print a corporate photo of the Peace of Mind Alarm Company logo," Gus told Luigi

"OK Boss," Luigi replied, as he started to walk away to make an instant start.

"Luigi," Gus shouted, Luigi, stopped and turned to listen to Gus. "It needs to happen tomorrow," Gus said.

Gus then went to Pitt and told him what he needed to do. Pitt knew he had already let down Paul Jones by saying as much as he had. He also knew that if he didn't oblige the steam iron torture and furnace were back on the agenda.

"If I do this, I want your word that O'Neill and I walk free after it's over?" Pitt told Gus.

"You have my word," Gus replied, that was good enough for Pitt.

Pitt's mobile phone rang out, the name on the screen showed, Nelly. "Nelly, its Steve here, how are things going?" Nelly is the nickname for the leader of the unit whose real name was Neven Novak, a loyal, tough, Croatian foot soldier who had been with for the family for fifteen years, he knew Pitt well and trusted him.

"Things are going well Steve." Gus could hear the voice through Pitt's earpiece, it was a strong Eastern European voice.

Nelly continued, "We are looking after the girl well, as you asked Steve. She isn't eating much and is feisty, but overall no problems, everything is going to plan."

"Have you spoke to her father?" Pitt asked trying to make I sound as natural as possible.

"Yes, he says he is trying all he can to get the money for the nineteenth. I am confident he has not got the police involved."

"Nelly the reason for the call is I want to make sure if things go against plan, and I am sure they won't," Pitt said.

"I want to make sure you have any warnings, so before Friday comes around I have arranged an alarm engineer to check everything over, He will come from the Peace of Mind Alarm Company, he has been checked out and it's Ok to let him in."

"And what about the Girl?" Nelly asked.

"I would want her safe and unseen whilst he is there, do you have somewhere to put her?"

"Yes, we can move her from the second sitting room to one of the bedrooms."

"Great," said Pitt, you are doing a great job, Nelly, catch up with you soon."

The phone went dead, and a bonus for Gus, he now knew Emily was in the second sitting room.

"Well done," Gus said to Pitt as he confiscated his mobile phone again.

***

December 16th. Lymm Cheshire.

Jonty arrived just outside Lymm, Cheshire at Giovanni's home. It was a large Edwardian detached house with four windows along the first floor and along the ground floor, sat precisely below the windows above. They were all large windows with panels in that made up of sixteen smaller, windows. The frames were painted brilliant white.

Jonty drove up the crescent-shaped gravelled drive in the Volvo before pulling it to rest next to the Mercedes AMG, which Jonty presumed was Giovanni's.

He walked up the drive. It was lined with seven-foot-high copper beech bushes, which at this time of year sat with the beautiful crisp deep brown leaves. These were similar to the outside of the house perimeters.

Jonty arrived at the black painted thick door, which had white painted panels inset. It sat in a brick porch with an apex slate roof matching the roof of the house.

The door was opened by Toni who looked tired, her eyes darkened following the crying following the death of Roberto.

"Good to see you again Detective," Toni said with the slightest of Italian accents, that she never lost, despite living in the UK for four decades.

Jonty entered a large hallway, with a large staircase boasting a spindled oak rail on both sides of the stairs, these lead to the first floor. The hallway tiling was maroon and cream and set in a diagonal diamond shape.

Toni took Jonty's overcoat from him and hung it on the coat rail attached to a wall with eight-period hangers on it.

She led Jonty through to the library where Giovanni sat waiting in a large, antique green leather chair next to a large well-lit, high flamed, cackling fire, throwing a welcome warmth at Jonty, a walking stick resting on the side of the chair following Giovanni's injuries at the funeral.

Toni offered to make a drink and left for the kitchen.

"Jonty, good to see you, I hear you had an experience with Gus and the boys in des-Moines."

Jonty's mind instantly visualised the steam iron on Fitzroy and the putrid smell of burning body smells escaping from the furnace. A memory Jonty would remember for the rest of his life.

Jonty sat in a matching chair on the other side of the fireplace with the hearth and a deep red and green flowered rug between them.

"What can I do for you Jonty? It seemed important on the phone earlier."

"We have an issue regarding timings Giovanni," Jonty replied, before continuing.

"I am staying in Richmond where I have located Paul and Quinn they are living under false names, Robert Green, and Colin Ashton,"

Giovanni gave a wry smile.

"I am trying to co-ordinate with Gus and the boys in Des-Moines. We have agreed to hit the house where Emily is held and the two houses of Quinn and Jones at the same time, we felt this was the best plan so one side could not tip off the other if we hit them separately." Jonty told Giovanni.

"That makes sense and how can I help?" Giovanni asked.

"I have tried doing it the legal way, this morning through the superintendent or North Yorkshire and he told me because of barriers he could not do it until mid-January, as you know it needs to be done by Friday the nineteenth, that's two days after tomorrow."

Giovanni, looked at the fire and spoke without making eye contact, "So you need my men to assist?"

"Yes if possible," Jonty replied.

"It will be headline news, Jonty and you may lose your job, or worse get prosecuted for your part," Giovanni explained.

"I know," Jonty said, "I have thought of that, a lot. Let us worry about that afterwards."

"I will do what I can Jonty, but you have left me with very little time, leave it with me," Giovanni replied.

They drank the tea Toni made along with scones with jam and cream, whilst they they spoke generally for fifteen minutes, mainly about Giovanni's injuries and operation.

Jonty left to make the three and a half-hour drive back to the hotel in Richmond, he did not want to be far away from Quinn and Jones.

CHAPTER TWENTY-NINE.

December 17th. Richmond.

Jonty rose early, he ate a full English breakfast which filled him full of energy, the jet lag from flying to America and back had now worn off. He dressed casually for the day, a pair of cream Chinos and a mid-blue crinoline shirt, Helen hated it, because it crumpled so much, it never looked ironed, a pair of brown shoes and a brown belt finished off his look.

He planned to look at the houses of Quinn and Jones, to see if anything would spring out to help with the strike as planned for Friday at 8.am UK time and Thursday three am in Des-Moines.

As he sat in the Volvo looking at the property owned by Jones, he saw an attractive woman walk from the property with a plastic bin bag in her hand, she walked to the bin and placed the bag in it. No mistaking the woman, this was Maggie Jones, Paul's wife.

He saw her mouth moving as she walked back towards the door, he could not hear what she was saying, as she reached the door, a smiling face came to edge of the threshold, Paul Jones. Now a certainty his work had come to fruition.

He reselected his satellite navigation system and cleared Waterfall House, owned by Jones and replaced it with Ripon Rise, the house owned by Quinn.

He could see why the two chose this area it was stunning with the freshly laid snow all around the landscape, the fields stretched for miles. Within two minutes, he arrived at Ripon Rise.

He could see a large front door, mainly made of glass, he could see through it as it covered two-thirds of the gable end. It was a well-presented barn conversion, popular in this area. He could see a body through a door, which was ajar. The house was very open and plain. After ten minutes, the body walked through the lounge door and into the spacious light wood, modern hallway, no doubting it. Quinn.

Jonty's work was complete for the morning. He planned in the afternoon to look at the photographs he took and try to set a strategy in place for the attack, this would not be easy as he had two properties to cover and run it in line with Des-Moines.

***

December 17th Des-Moines.

Luigi pulled the white Nissan NV200 compact cargo van into the yard of Tommy Deluisi. Tommy was good at what he did, which was mainly, any print job. Luigi asked for the Peaceful Alarm Company logo in vinyl that would stick easily to the side, but not with a resin that would permanently keep it adhered, as it would need to, be peeled off again that evening, as it would be needed again for future jobs. Luigi did not want paint from the van coming off with it. Luigi had asked at 3.00 pm the previous day and wanted it by 8.00 am today.

"Tommy, how are you doing?" Luigi asked.

"Are we ready to do business?" Luigi asked.
"Just about, I was working until four in the morning to get the vinyl logo's ready," Tommy said.
"And worth every penny of the two grand we are paying you, Tommy." They both laughed and Luigi patted Tommy on the back, then walked back to the van and drove it into the garage.
"It's warm in here Tommy, thanks for thinking of me," Luigi said.
"It's not for you Luigi it is to get the vinyl on the van." Luigi laughed, he knew that.
Tommy began by thoroughly cleaning one side of the panels of the van, and into any indents and crevices, he could see.
He looked at the temperature on the wall gauge it read seventy-two degrees. Within the optimum range of seventy to eighty degrees, knowing if he goes too high it will make the vinyl to soft, and colder will make the vinyl too rigid and would be difficult to apply.
Tommy used a tape measure to help with the positioning and put masking tape around the area he wanted to work. Tommy peeled the back paper off, small areas at a time, he began to place it on the side of the van, using an air release tool for excess bubbles, it took an hour adhering a small piece at a time. Eventually it was complete. Finally, he trimmed any excess with a razor knife and repeated it on the other side.
He picked up a paint gun with a mixture of oil, grease, and a small amount of grey paint. He then sprayed it over a few random parts of the sign, he wiped down with a dirty cloth. Instantly, the sign aged five years.

  Luigi left the garage at eleven twenty and made his way to willow barn, he drove down the cobbled road and turned into the large wrought iron gates, which were, open for him, as he was expected.

He knocked on the door, a large barrel-chested man, six feet six inches tall, and weighing two hundred and sixty pounds with not an ounce of fat on him asked Luigi in an East European accent.

"Can I help you?" the man asked.

"I am here to look at the alarm system." Luigi replied, although his white overalls had, 'The Peace of Mind Alarm Company' emblazoned on them and the van parked, purposefully placed behind him.

"Luigi walked in carrying a canvas long bag with all the tools he required to meet his task.

The East European showed Luigi into the main sitting room, where another thug-like man was reading a magazine, he never raised his head to acknowledge. Luigi was happy with this. *If you do not look, you do not see.* Luigi thought, not wanting publicity.

He looked at the system, there was an audio alarm, he double-checked his notes.

"It says here to have all alarms silent. Surely that isn't right?" Luigi asked.

"If that's what it says, that's what it says, do it." The European answered.

Luigi had no such instruction but it suited to have them silent on Friday.

He went to the second sitting room and saw a camera pointing directly at a comfortable armchair.

That must be where they are keeping Emily, Luigi thought instantly. *If they used the system as intended, it would point towards the door, not an armchair.* He thought it through.

"I just need my ladders, to check that camera," Luigi said.

He returned a couple of minutes later with a pair of ladders and quickly climbed them to the camera, undid it, and looked inside, he played around with it for a while then came down, he looked at the remainder of the system and left the property.

"How did it go?" Gus asked Luigi as he walked into the room.

"It went well. I have something to show you." Luigi replied.

The two men walked over to the corner of the annexe, Luigi picked up his laptop computer on the way over. He opened the lid and started dialling into the internet, he pressed a few more buttons.

"All this technology, it's beyond me." Gus said, "Give me a gun and a knife and I'm happy." He continued.

"You're a dinosaur." Luigi laughed.

After a minute or so a picture came up on the screen, of a woman sat reading in an armchair.

"Very good, does she tell us a story now?" Gus asked not understanding the gravity.

"That's a live feed on Emily, that's Emily right now," Luigi said.

"Whilst I was checked the system, I noticed this particular camera aimed at the chair and not the door, I guessed that was where Emily is kept so they can keep an eye on her even when they are not in the room," Luigi told Gus.

"Fantastic, Luigi," Gus told him.

"Also I have set the alarm so the bell will not ring, so in effect, it's null and void, and finally, the two cameras that were on the corners of the wall, I have set a timer so they will disable at two am Friday morning."

"You're a genius," Gus told him.

"I know he replied, can I have a pay rise?"

"No!" Gus answered. They both laughed.

Gus allowed Jake to look at the live stream of Emily, in the armchair, through the camera Luigi had reset for their benefit, Jake watched as anger welled up inside. He could see she was well looked after, for now, however, the reality was. His wife had been kidnapped.

CHAPTER THIRTY

December 18th, Richmond

Jonty devoured the same breakfast he had chosen the previous morning, a full English breakfast, he chose, two eggs, three rashers of bacon, three sausages, fried mushrooms, baked beans, and two hash browns, he smothered it in ketchup and ate it with two rounds of toast. Helen would be furious at his large helping. *Make hay whilst the sun shines.* Jonty thought.

Jonty relaxed after his breakfast with a large mug of coffee, in what now was becoming his favourite place in the hotel, the armchair in front of the ever-burning fire.

As he sat thinking how he would manage planning the strike on Jones and Quinn the following day his phone light began flashing with the familiar, basic, ring tone following immediately. He looked at the incoming call, the name read, Giovanni.

"Giovanni, how are you?" Jonty welcomed him.

"I am very well, thank you, Jonty, however, I have some bad news." Giovanni's voice appeared quieter than normal.

The phone went silent for a few seconds before Giovanni continued. "Jonty, I am not going to be of assistance tomorrow, I cannot muster a team strong enough for tomorrow, evening."

"Giovanni do not tell me this, I need it you know it lines up with the Des-Moines operation. The timing needs to be precise."

"Jonty I know. My men are scattered all over Europe, following the death of Roberto and, the attack on me, it made sense to scatter the team in case other attacks were planned. I did it to protect the family. Now we cannot get everybody back by tomorrow. There are no flight availabilities. They are all fully booked as everyone is flying home for Christmas."

Jonty went quiet before Giovanni continued. "I may be able to get one maybe two back but that won't help. If it was after Christmas it would be fine if anything changes I will call you Jonty, but as it stands now we cannot assist. I am sorry Jonty."

Giovanni, in Giovanni's style, ended the call there. Jonty stared at the phone for thirty seconds as if by magic a solution would appear, it did not.

Jonty looked at the floor for five minutes considering his options. He concluded he did not have many.

He picked up his phone and rang Superintendent Morris. He felt a little uncomfortable making the call but had no option. He knew that many of his colleagues were on Billy's payroll. He concealed some relevant points from Morris, because of this. Particularly after discovering Quinn and Shepherd were, 'bent coppers.'

"Jonty how are things?" Morris asked.

"Fine thank you, sir, I thought it was a good point in the proceedings to give you an update." Jonty lied.

He told Morris about his meeting with Superintendent Miller and that he could not assist until mid-January. He also told him that he had physically seen Jones and Quinn.

"That makes perfect sense to me Jonty, let's go through the proper channels and I will give you all the support you need, then you, Miller, and I, can attack this for all it is worth."

Jonty had to think on his feet, he could not tell Morris about Gus's operation in Des-Moines, or the fact that he had been in discussion with Giovanni. He was in a tight corner.

"Under normal circumstances, I would agree to sir, but on this occasion, we have Jones and Quinn within touching distance. I fear we will lose them, they will move on. We may never get this chance again."

"Ok," Morris went silent. "What do you need Jonty?" Morris asked after a few seconds.

"I need to survey the two properties. I need at least five men. That would be three men per property, more if possible. I would like to enter the properties and place both Jones and Quinn under arrest on the suspicion of, murder, money laundering, kidnap, drug trafficking, arms trafficking, and anything else we can lay at their doorstep."

"When do you intend to do this Jonty?"

"Tomorrow at 8.00 am sir."

"Jonty, we would be doing this against protocol and it could go badly wrong. It's too little time to plan."

"I know sir, but it's too big an opportunity to miss."

"Leave it with me Jonty, I am not promising anything but leave it with me."

"Thank you, sir." Is all Jonty could say.

Two hours later Jonty's phone rang. It was Morris.

"Jonty I managed to get a search warrant from the Magistrates court. I told them the importance and gave them basic details. I think the fact that Quinn was involved helped to swing it."

"Thank you, sir," Jonty replied, "And men?"

"I have a car with three men in on its way to Richmond as we speak," Morris replied.

Morris was delivering, not quite enough men, but delivering.

"Because of the short notice I asked for volunteers, I got three, Bill Jordan, Grant Bell, and Frank Rose," Morris added.

"Thank you, sir. I will bring them up to speed later when they arrive."

"Don't let me down Jonty, we all want Quinn to stand trial," Morris said.

"Thank you, sir, I won't let you down."

Jonty put the phone down, not a perfect preparation, but a chance, all he needed was a chance!

***

Des-Moines December 18th

Gus assembled the team in the conference room at the Newark Liberty International airport hotel.

They sat at a ten-foot-long table with a pristine white tablecloth on it, on top of the table were several iced jugs of water, hot coffee and several types of fruit juice along with sandwiches, cakes, biscuits and chocolate bars to snack on.

Gus put the plans through a laptop computer, it showed the images on the screen. He began with the photographs, taken by Luigi and the overhead helicopter.

He told them how they would enter the building through the front and the rear.

He told them he expected two teams, a team of four resting and a team of three guarding Emily.

He split his men into two teams. Gus would lead one team: Freddie, Piero, Santi, Nani, and Jake.

Luigi would lead a second team: Alessandro, Jim Boy, Calvin 'Calv' Hewitt, and Kev Dore, both drafted in for the job.

That makes us a team of nine against seven. We need to work fast and effectively. It is not important to take prisoners. The object is to get Emily out of there safe. He looked at Jake, who returned the acknowledgment with a nervous smile.

He outlined the plan in minute detail. Gus passed the second part of the presentation to Luigi, he confirmed the alarm bells were eliminated from the system, Emily could be seen at all times through the laptop, the images were being monitored in the van by Red. Mick O'Malley was the family technology expert, with an Irish background and flaming red hair he was the only Irishman employed by the family, and drafted in with Calv and Kev.

***

Richmond December 18th, 5.30 PM.

At five-thirty Bill Jordan, Grant Bell and Frank Rose arrived at The Frenchgate Hotel. Jonty knew all three men well.

Bill Jordan had been in the force for twenty years plus. He had been a partner of Jonty for two years, they took on the Manchester criminals with a smile on their face, they both loved to fight. They never let each other down and once, stood back to back against eight, baton and knife, wielding youths for ten minutes until backup arrived to help them.

"Bill it's great to see you, what made you volunteer," Jonty asked.

"Jonty I owe you a lot, old times, all mixed into one. I want to help you get this sorted." He replied.

Grant Bell was the next to shake hands. Bell had been an officer for around five years, held in high esteem by Superintendent Quinn, he was quickly promoted through the ranks to Detective Inspector, over quickly some thought.

Jonty was one of these, and the first thing that crossed Jonty's mind was whether he was a Quinn recruit. He wondered if he might be on the 'payroll' of Jones and Quinn. However he needed all the support he could get at this point, but he would be wary of Bell.

"Grant good to see you, Thanks for coming along," Jonty said with a smile, covering his concerns.

The third volunteer was Frank Rose, a 'bobby on the beat' constable who Jonty first met as a wet behind the ears recruit, Jonty thought back to the first time they met.

Jonty was at a point where he was closing in on the black BMW that had killed Paul Jennings. He had booked a car from the police pool car system to travel from Manchester to Birmingham, following a lead Jonty had, and a driver. The driver was Frank.

He remembered the day well.

Jonty left for the station as planned just after 7 am. The twenty-minute drive was straightforward before the usual morning traffic build-up started. He arrived at the station to find a fresh-faced constable sitting at the vacant desk next to Jonty's, feet up and coffee in hand. Jonty walked up to him and, with a firm hand, swiped his legs so they fell off the desk and to the floor, the coffee spilling on the desk and between the constable's legs. He shot up, making sure the coffee had not spilled on his uniform.

"Don't ever let me see you slouch in a uniform, lad, in or out of sight of the public," said Jonty. "I suppose you are the person travelling with me to Birmingham?"

"Yes, sir. PC Frank Rose."

Jonty shook his hand. "Okay, Frank. I am not sure you look old enough to drive – can you?"

Frank felt under pressure and wanted to impress the detective, whom he had heard so much about.

"Yes, sir," said Rose. "I'm twenty-five and I have a license."

"Great," said Jonty. "You drive."

Five minutes passed and they were in the car park. The department released a grey Volvo V40 estate car for them. *Comfortable enough*, thought Jonty.

Frank slowly eased the car out of the Salford compound and onto the M602, about two hundred yards away. The car, used for motorway patrolling, was unmarked. It had blue flashing lights under the front grill if required and its three-litre engine would keep up with most speeding cars, at the junction before the entrance of the motorway, the car stopped suddenly. Jonty and Frank surged forward like torpedoes protected only by their seat belts.

"What are you doing?" asked Jonty in surprise.

"Sorry, sir, I forgot it was an automatic," said Frank.

Frank had naturally tried to depress the clutch pedal to change gear. However, in the absence of the clutch, he had slammed on the oversized brake pedal instead, causing the car to do an emergency-style stop.

"Did you say your name was Frank Spencer?" Jonty asked sarcastically, using the name of the Michael Crawford TV accident-prone, character.

"No, sir, it's Frank Rose," said the constable. "I don't know a Frank Spencer. Is he in the force?"

Jonty rolled his eyes. "No, I don't think so. Let's get there in one piece, Frank!".

Jonty took Frank under his wing following an accident, directly related to Paul Jones.

Jonty was on the stakeout at Billy Jones' house, the day Quinn planned the escape. Unbeknown to Jonty, Frank was on duty at the scene, he saw what happened.

A black Lexus travelled down the road where Paul Jones lived, Jonty had already parked in time to watch it all unfold.

The Lexus drove past Jonty's CRV, approximately fifty yards from the gates of the Jones house, a uniformed officer walked out and raised his right arm, requesting the vehicle to stop. However, instead of slowing down, the car accelerated. The officer tried jumping out of the way of the oncoming vehicle, the car caught him, he was launched ten feet in the air.

The officer fell to the ground with a thud. His knee bent, in the opposite direction it was designed to bend. His arms were twisted and contorted on the floor, his head rolling to the side. Jonty ran up to the officer to help. Jonty looked down. He recognised the face. PC Frank Rose, the outrageously innocent bobby he came to know and love over the previous months. He felt for a pulse – there was one, albeit a very faint.

"He needs an ambulance!" Jonty shouted. "He is still alive." He watched his controlled fingers, as if in slow motion, dial 999.

Over the following months of Frank's rehabilitation, Jonty became closer to Frank, when Frank returned to work, initially on light duties they lunched together in the canteen. Jonty helped Frank become the police constable he is today, not perfect, but a lot further down the road than the initial trip to Birmingham.

Jonty knew exactly why Frank was here. Loyalty, and an injury to settle with Billy.

Jonty returned to his room after chatting to everybody generally and told them he would outline the detail over their evening meal.

They returned to go to their rooms at six pm. Jonty used the first-hour showering and talking to Helen on the phone.

The second hour Jonty utilised thinking of a realistic working plan to the following morning.

The first thing he thought was to set them in teams of two, one team for Jones, one for Quinn.

He had total confidence for the reasons Jordan and Frank were there, loyalty, friendship and genuinely wanting to help Jonty out.

He worried until his stomach churned about Grant Bell. There was no history between Bell and himself. He was mentored by Quinn, in the past, *Why?* Jonty thought.

There is no reason for Bell to volunteer. He thought.

He thought of the adage, *keep your friends close, and your enemies closer.*

The first decision made, Frank would work with Jordan and Jonty with Bell, allowing Jonty to keep an eye on Bell.

This made the second decision easy, Keep Bell away from Quinn. Jordan and Frank would survey Quinn whilst Bell and Jonty would survey Jones.

So far so good, Jonty thought. *The teams need to act simultaneously he knew that was 8.00 am, but how?* The next question arose.

They parked half a mile away from each property and walked the remaining distance, the risk to this was being seen by either Jones or Quinn, a small risk and one worth taking. Jonty loaded two police battering rams, called the enforcer, known informally by the force as "the big red key" in the Volvo when he picked it up knowing he would need to break into the houses. They would have to walk the distance, although, in casual clothes, they would need to carry an enforcer between each team, the ones chosen by Jonty were steel cylindrical and had two handles on it to allow one person, leverage to open any domestic door easily. The risk again, they may be seen, the advantage being, at this time of year, the walk would be under the cover of darkness.

They would arrive at the properties around seven-thirty am, use the thirty minutes to survey any activity, from the homes, and make a live assessment there and then. The rule was, however, that they do strike regardless. That was imperative.

Apart from truncheons, the teams had no weaponry, guns not allowed, none of the team had firearm licenses.

They had their evening meal and all were clear about the task ahead.

Jonty told them, "We convene in the breakfast room of the hotel at six am sharp. A quick breakfast then we set off at six-thirty on the dot." Jonty received three nods.

By ten pm the meal had finished, no alcohol had been consumed, they were professional. They all retired for a good night's sleep before the task ahead.

Jonty's final task was to phone Gus, They discussed each other's plan and both confirmed they were ready to activate them.

"Good luck Gus." Jonty said, "And to you my friend." Gus replied.

Jonty settled into bed at ten-thirty and found sleep very easy.

CHAPTER THIRTY-ONE

Richmond December 19th, 6.45 AM

After breakfast they walked out to the cars, the night had been cold, the sky was black with every star sparkling. A clear night with no clouds meant only one thing, cold temperatures. The temperature was minus five degrees, the underlying snow was hard and icy. They needed to be careful as they stepped along the pathway. Jonty removed one of the battering rams from the Volvo and gave it to Frank and Jordan, they loaded the Vauxhall Cavalier police pool car they travelled in and climbed into it. Jonty and Bell entered the Volvo ready to drive to the properties.

Both cars fired up the lights lit up the otherwise dark car-park at the hotel and they slowly moved to the job at hand.

It took fifteen minutes for the both cars to be in position. They parked on the verge centrally between the two properties. They took out the battering rams and shook hands all wishing each other good luck.

They were in position early at around seven twenty-five, as agreed, they sat in their teams at front of the two properties, the lights at Jones's house were all switched off and it was very quiet.

Jonty and Bell settled down on the opposite side of the lane behind a bramble hedge with a convenient space in it to pass through. They watched, all was quiet, Billy and Maggie were asleep.

At Ripon Rise, where Quinn lived, Jordan and Frank were in position.

"Just keep looking and listening Jordan said to Frank." He noticed Frank was a little nervous. Frank nodded back.

Jordan and Frank were just beyond the grass verge under the cover of a well-established six-foot-high private hedge. The lights were on, probably a habit from years of Quinn being used to a structured life in the police force.

***

Richmond. December 19th, 8.00 am.

"Let's go," Jordan whispered to Frank.

They crept up the driveway of Ripon house. Jordan knew the easiest way to enter a property was with the least resistance. He knocked on the door, all stayed quiet. He knocked again, again nothing.

He turned to the enforcer, took the cylinder in both hands and held tight on to the handles, he swung akin to how a golfer would swing a golf club, he had been taught, it's not the power it's the technique, it hit the door full blast, it moved but did not open. He swung again faster this time. *It is not force it is the technique,* he told himself, it splintered. A third swing and the door broke from the lock, it was bolted at the top and the bottom. The bottom stayed in place the top falling by gravity as the central portion of the door splintered and broke sending dark green painted shards of wood in all directions.

As they entered the property, a slamming door was heard.

"He's gone out of the back door," Jordan shouted, they both sprinted to the back of the house, they opened the back door and ran into the cold air, they could see a tall wooden gate attached to a drystone wall swinging open, they rushed to it,

"Left or right?" Frank asked Jordan.

"You go left I go right," was the reply.

"They both sprinted in opposite directions. The sky was now turning grey with a sprinkle of daylight shining through. It was a silhouette, no more, definitely a man running, he was fifty yards away, Frank upped his speed a little, he could see the man was not running as fast as he was, probably due to age, a twenty-five-year-old man would expect to outrun a man in his late fifties.

"JORDAN!" Frank shouted,

"I'M COMING!" was the reply from around one-hundred yards in the opposite direction.

The man was markedly slowing down. Frank was only thirty yards away when suddenly the man turned around. Frank recognised him. It was Quinn.

Quinn raised both arms, Frank could tell the shape in the shadows of the morning. "HE HAS A GUN!" Frank shouted, just as he heard the crack come from the barrel, Frank dived to the left into a bush that was in the field, there was a scattering of bushes all over the field. The sheep in the field started bolting at the sound of the gun.

"STAY WHERE YOU ARE!" Quinn shouted towards Frank.

Frank stayed low, Quinn turned and carried on in the direction he started. Frank left the bush and followed. Quinn stopped and turned again aware that Frank was still following him.

He raised the gun again, another crack from the barrel, Frank heard a nearby tree receive the bullet, it couldn't have missed Frank by much.

"I'M WARNING YOU!" Quinn shouted again. "STAY WHERE YOU ARE!"

Just as he spoke, Frank saw a body dive out of the hedges at the side of Quinn and onto him. It was Jordan, who had diverted around the back of the hedge and tracked on the blindside until he saw an opening.

The two men wrestled, Quinn still had the gun in his hand, Frank reached the scene seconds later kicking Quinn's arm, the gun flew out of his hand settling five metres away.

Quinn and Jordan were punching each other with Quinn holding his own against a man his own age. Frank kicked Quinn in the face, his nose gave way and a stream of deep red blood flew from his nostrils leaving a line across his cheek. Frank kicked him again, this time it landed in the mouth, Quinn was wobbling he spat out a tooth, Jordan again dived on Quinn, there was not much resistance this time, he took out his handcuffs and clasped one tightly around Quinn's wrist, quickly, he pulled the other arm around his back and clasped that. Quinn was now handcuffed and secure.

All three men were breathing heavily. Jordan turned Quinn over onto his back and sat on him. Quinn started chattering and shaking with the cold, as he lay forced on his back on ice and snow, he was wearing a pair of slippers pyjamas and an overcoat he managed to grab on his way out.

"I am arresting you for murder, money laundering, drug trafficking, aiding and abetting, kidnap, obstruction in preventing the police carry to out inquiries, oh and resisting arrest. You do not have to say anything, but it may harm your defence if you do not mention when questioned something, which you later rely on in court." Jordan gave Quinn his rights.

He dragged him up from the snow before frog-marching him back to the Cavalier.

***

As 8.00 am struck, Waterfall House, the Jones home, was still in complete darkness, Billy was still in bed, making the job a little easier for Jonty and Bell.

Jonty turned to Bell and whispered, "Let's go."

As the words came out, Jonty felt a prick in the back of his neck, he wiped it with his hand, at first thinking it was a thorn, he went light-headed, then he wobbled and fell to the ground on his knees. He was dazed but still had the presence to think. *Bell I knew it!* A few seconds later, he leaned forward then, DARKNESS!

***

Des-Moines. December 19th. 2 am.

Gus assembled the team in the warehouse and ensured they all knew what their role was in the job they were about to undertake. They did.

The first team, named team one, were Freddie, Piero, Santi, Nani, and Jake. Climbed into a BMW MX5, followed by, team two. Alessandro, Jim Boy, Calvin 'Calv' Hewitt, and Kev Dore in the second MX5.

Gus travelled with Luigi in the van Red would be monitoring from, Red was driving, Gus and Luigi sat in the back of the van finalising the plan, no mistakes could be made, this was a plan that if one-minute detail went a miss it could cost any one of their lives.

They arrived at Willow Barn around 2.30 am. A quick text to Jonty saying they were there on schedule. A return from Jonty saying it was 7.30 Am UK time, and all was on schedule there as well.

The clock crept to 7.45 am. Gus slid back the side-panelled door on the van and stepped into the dark cold night, followed by Luigi. Red left the front of the van and entered the ear via the sliding door. He sat in a grey office style chair and began to fire up the computers. "They will be live in five minutes he told Gus."

"Good that will be plenty of time" Gus replied.

Gus looked up to the roof and team two were in place, he could see the silhouetted bodies waiting for the signal at 8.00 am.

He looked towards the side of the building from ground level, he could see the shape of Piero, just ahead of the bushes that lined down the side of the barn, the remainder of team one hid within the bushes behind Piero.

At 7.50 am, Luigi took the shoulder-fired rocket launcher, or bazooka as it was also known, from the back of the van, he loaded it with a shell. The unguided rocket launcher was set and ready with five minutes to spare.

The synchronized watches hit 8.00 am. Luigi took aim and fired the bazooka at the upstairs window, the window he knew the men slept from his visit two days earlier.

Luigi pulled the trigger, he jerked backward as the recoil from the gun told him the shell had launched, it whistled through the air, and both teams knew the operation had begun.

Within a second, the shell smashed through the window, an orange light lit up the room for a second, smoke-filled out of the open space along with glass shards omitted like a tropical rainstorm, fast, furious and heavy.

This was the sign for the teams to act. Team two abseiled from the roof and swung into the glass free bedroom window. They had gas masks on and threw tear gas canisters in the room. One man lay dead from the bazooka, another dazed and two no longer in the room, they fled into the house, Alessandro aimed his Ruger SR9c pistol at the dazed man and pulled the trigger. Alessandro liked the Ruger because it is compact with full-size capabilities. A magazine capacity of 17 rounds.

"Two down, five to go, two from upstairs have fled the room," Alessandra shouted down his speaker allowing the rest of the teams to hear on the headphones they were wearing.

The second team advanced through the bedroom door, a volley of bullets came at them striking Jim Boy in the shoulder.

"Man down!" Alessandro shouted down the microphone.

Team one by now had sledgehammered through the patio doors and were downstairs, standing behind walls protecting themselves from the volley of fire from the three men guarding Emily, Piero knew they could not fire randomly for fear of hitting Emily.

"Three men in the downstairs room," Red shouted down the microphone, watching it unfold on the screen. "The girl is in too much danger to return fire, repeat do not return fire!"

"We are not strong enough against them!" Piero shouted from behind the wall, "outside now!" Team one ran back through the patio doors they entered minutes before.

Upstairs the gunshots quenched, the tear gas had done the job and the remaining two kidnappers were now unconscious on the floor. Team two walked up to them and filled them with around thirty bullets as the bodies danced into death-like marionettes.

Downstairs team one retreated, sprinting out of the building. The kidnappers followed, filled with confidence, knowing they were superior to their attackers.

As the room emptied, Jake strolled in with wire cutters in his hand. Emily looked through the smoke left by the gunfire and instantly recognised her husband. Jake put his finger vertically to his lips, showing the sign for Em to be quiet.

He cut the chains attaching the handcuffs to the chair, she was free, she was sobbing uncontrollably, Em was shaking. Jake put the palms of his hands up, motioning her not to move. She nodded.

Jake walked back towards the forced patio doors and checked all was clear. It was, he walked back to Em and took her by the hand leading her through the doors, as he did one of the men saw Jake and ran towards him wielding a knife, Jake pushed Em back into the room, The man swung the knife in a horizontal plane, throat high. Jake dropped his body to floor level and scythed a kick bringing the man down. Jake sprung back up with a handspring and hit the man flush in the face with the heel of his boot. He gripped the man's knife and had it above his head ready for the downward thrust.

"No Jake!" he recognised Em's voice.

"Don't kill him!" Jake stopped,

Jake looked at Em and shook his head in agreement. He kicked the man in the face until he was unconscious. Jake looked around and saw a long electric wire connecting the lamp at the side of Em's chair to an electrical wall socket. He unplugged the socket, took the wire cutters, before cutting each end of the wire before tying the unconscious man's hands behind his back.

He took Em's hand, they walked out of the building crouching.

"Emily is free and another enemy hit, tied but not dead," Jake said down the microphone.

"Two remaining, well done Jake," Gus responded.

"Make that one!" the familiar voice of Luigi came through.

Team one planned to leave the building in the hope that the kidnappers would follow, leaving it free for Jake to release Em. They did.

Teams, one and two joined forces outside the barn and surrounded the kidnappers, a gun battle pursued, Luigi had done his work, the plan to take them behind a garage outbuilding worked to perfection, they had the cover they required and the kidnappers were exposed in the open fields.

"No more enemy in sight," Luigi added.

"A kidnapper has re-entered the building," Red shouted as he saw a body enter the sitting room.

"I am the nearest I will go," Gus told the teams.

He quickly arrived at the barn and entered. Stood there was Neven 'Nelly' Novak. The two men looked like two heavyweight boxers stood ready for a title fight.

"Nelly, long time no see," Gus said to the Croatian giant.

"Gus, the last time I saw you we were allies fighting together in a turf war for the drugs in New York."

"You were a Sartori family member then Nelly, not a splinter group supporter!"

"A man has to earn a living," Nelly replied.

"Facing the Sartori, Abano and Mainiero families is not a way to make a living, dying is no living Nelly," Gus replied.

Nelly shrugged his shoulders and smiled.

Alessandro and Luigi entered the room.

"This is nothing to do with you, it's Gus and Me," Nelly said to the newcomers.

"Nelly, I will spare your life, if you give me your word not to work for Billy Jones anymore, his days are numbered, come and work for me? We have lost a good man Luca, he needs replacing. Jim Boy is hit and we don't know if he will live. It's time to come home."

"I can't do that Gus."

"I know." Gus Replied, admiring, the loyalty.

Nelly put his hand inside, his black leather jacket, Gus did the same, Nelly gained the split second required to expose his gun first, he aimed it at Gus, Gus felt a force from his right. Alessandro dived on Gus pushing him to the floor just as Nelly fired his Smith & Wesson, Luigi drew his gun and hit Nelly in the chest, Luigi was always, taught to aim for the largest part of the body, and Nelly's chest was ample. Then a follow-up shot landed in the forehead guaranteeing Nelly to be dead before his carcass hit the floor.

Gus turned to Alessandro. Alli, had been shot in the stomach.

"Alli, speak to me?" Gus ordered.

"Gus I love you, and I have enjoyed every minute of our friendship."

"Alli do not die, keep fighting!" Gus demanded. Alessandro, was by now cradled in Gus's arms.

"Luca, I can see Luca, he is calling me. Live long and well my friend," were Alessandro's final words.

His body went limp in Gus's arms.

"When are we going to learn, this is a mug's game!" Gus said to Luigi, who stayed quiet with a tear in his eye.

The journey back was quiet. Gus broke the silence. "Two men lost in several days and one badly injured all because of a man who could not correctly manage his family. Billy Jones! I pray to god Jonty has done his job."

In the second BMW, Em was crying with shock, and trembling as she tucked into Jake's chest.

Jake kissed her on the forehead, "Shh it's all OK, it's all over now," he told her.

The cars slowly travelled back in a precession as if the funeral cars had arrived early.

CHAPTER THIRTY-TWO.

December 19th, 5.30 pm

Jonty woke to feel drowsy, he lay in a half-conscious state, his vision blurred, his senses told him he was warm, comfortable in bed and a head that hurt like an alarm clock ringing in his skull, never ceasing.

He shook his head, after a few minutes his vision began to return. He was in a large bedroom, he lay in a double bed with a cream thick duvet covering him, two, duck down pillows were cradling a head unable to raise more than a few inches. The room was dark, he looked at his watch it read 5.30. He knew it would be dark outside. A lamp sat on an expensive-looking bedside table He extended his arm from the warm duvet, reached to turn the light switch on. The light made his eyes squint, a few minutes later they adjusted to the light.

The bedroom, designed with light green pastel-painted walls, a pure white ceiling, with deep covings. The ceilings were high, Jonty guessed around eleven foot, this made Jonty feel he was in a Victorian-style property. It had a cream carpet and a large, white ribbed, radiator, the type Jonty remembered in hospitals.

A knock on the door and a lady Jonty guessed in her mid-seventies walked through the door with a tray containing a bowl of vegetable soup, a large white mug of tea, Jonty could see the steam rising off it, and a glass of clear freshwater accompanying two paracetamol.

Jonty put the tablets in his mouth from the palm of his hand and drank the fresh cool water, the half-pint went down in one.

"Good evening, DI Ball, how are you feeling?" the woman asked.

"Where am I?" Jonty answered with a question.

"You don't have to worry about that DI Ball, you are safe." She handed a mobile phone to him.

"There are five minutes available on the phone, I have set your wife's name into it, I am sure she will be worried. Helen isn't it?"

"Where am I?" Jonty asked again.

"You have an en-suite bathroom in the corner." the lady nodded to a door in the corner of the room. "I will pick you up for your evening meal at six-thirty."

"WHERE AM I? WHO ARE YOU?" Jonty shouted, but feeling too weak to leave the bed.

"So six-thirty it is then!" She swiveled and walked out of the room. Jonty heard a key lock the door.

***

December 19th, 5.00 pm Manchester

Quinn sat in the interview room, he looked tired and disheveled, he had changed from his pyjama's to a light blue matching top and baggy linen trousers, supplied by his local hosts.

Quinn recognised the click of the familiar recording machine.

"My name is DI William Jordan, I am about to lead the Interview with ex-Superintendent John Quinn, regarding his arrest on the grounds of, murder, gun running, the attempted murder of a police officer, resisting arrest, and the kidnap DI Jonty Ball. With me in the room is PC Frank Rose. The time is 17.01 exactly."

"Where is DI Jonty Ball, Paul Jones, and his wife Maggie?" Jordan went straight for the kill.

"I don't know anything about it!" Quinn replied.

"So what you are saying is, your boss, Paul Jones, his wife Margaret, have escaped along with the disappearance of DI Jonty Ball? Who was leading a police operation, and you had no idea?"

"That is what I am saying," Quinn responded.

"Next question," Jordan said, "Do you know why DI Grant Bell was injected with a substance that made him unconscious and left on the roadside?"

"I know nothing about any of this, if I knew there was an operation in place, do you think I would have stayed around?" Quinn replied.

"I will not answer any questions without my solicitor being present." Quinn continued.

"As you wish," Jordan responded.

"The interview with ex-Superintendent John Quinn ended at 17.04 precisely" Jordan switched off the recorder and left the room with Frank, as they walked out they were replaced by a constable waiting outside the room.

Jordan and Frank drove over to Salford Royal Hospital, where DI Grant Bell, had been admitted. Jordan spoke to the ward Sister on the desk, before entering the ward. He showed her his card.

"It looks like he was administered a low dosage of Midazolam." The ward sister said reading from Bell's notes.

"What is Midazalem?" Jordan asked.

"Midazolam is a sedative, in a hospital situation, an anesthesiologist may administer when you are heading into surgery. It stops you from getting nervous about an operation looming. It does not put you to sleep as such, but you will feel sleepy and you will not remember anything that happens while the drug is in effect. In surgeries, you get midazolam first, and then the anaesthetic afterwards." The sister told Jordan and Frank.

"Thank you, sister. May we see him now?" Jordan asked.

"You may, he is in the third ward on the left."

"What went on out there Grant?" Jordan asked.

"Jonty and I were in position, he gave me the nod to proceed, the next thing I remember is waking up in this bed, apparently somebody called the ambulance, a good job they did or I would have caught hyperthermia," Bell answered.

"Do you know what happened to Jonty?" Jordan asked.

"No." Bell answered, "Is he not here, in a ward?"

"Nobody has seen him. I am worried, we started questioning Quinn and he swears he knew nothing about it." Frank added.

"You have Quinn?" Bell asked.

"Yes."

"What about Billy Jones?" Bell quizzed.

"He went missing along with his wife and Jonty. I think we should call him Houdini!" Jordan added.

***

December 19th, 6.30 pm.

The antique clock in the bedroom, Jonty occupied read 6.30 precisely. He felt better now the effect of the midazolam wore off. He showered before putting on a set of clothes left out for him,
Not my style, he thought.
A pair of navy blue trousers, a grey long-sleeved shirt, finished off with a pair of brown moccasins, but the fit was perfect. He was also aware they were new, obviously bought with Jonty in mind.
Jonty heard the key in the lock turn, he saw the door swing open, the same woman he met earlier stood there.
"Would you like to accompany me to the dining room DI Ball?"
Jonty rose from the armchair placed in the corner of the room and followed the woman out.
As he descended, the stairs there were two very large grand-looking dark oak doors, with large brass round handles, closed, with a butler stood in front of them. The butler, dressed in black except for a white dress shirt and a pair of white gloves, he opened the doors simultaneously. He was tall and slim with collar length grey hair, Jonty placed him at around seventy years of age.
Jonty entered the doors, only one man sat at the large twenty seat mahogany dining table. Giovanni!
"Jonty welcome, take a seat." I have ordered the best steak for our meal, I hope you approve?"
"GIOVANNI!" Jonty said in a loud voice.
"What is going on Giovanni?"
"Take a seat Jonty, I will explain as we eat," Giovanni said as he gestured with his hand for Jonty to take an adjacent seat.

***

Des-Moines 19th December. 3.30 pm.

Gus was disappointed in the day, he had lost two of his best men in two days. He spent $20,000 on the operation, all to help a friend out, Giovanni, although he knew Giovanni would cover the expense.

Jake left Em's side, walked over to Gus, shook his hand, and thanked him.

"What will you do from here?" Gus asked Jake.

"I think the first thing we will do is get Christmas back on track and take it from there. We fell in love with England when we were there eighteen-months ago, so we need to decide if to stay here or live in England, decisions that can wait." Jake answered.

"You?" He asked Gus.

"My first job is to tell Luca and Alli's family the bad news, what a Christmas present eh?"

"Luca had two children a boy and a girl, aged twelve and ten, I am the Godfather to Bobby, the youngest, and Alessandro was the godfather to Jenny, his daughter. Alli doted on that girl." Gus said with a voice full of remorse.

"Alli didn't have a family, that's why he was close to Luca and his family, they have a double whammy coming." Gus finished.

Em walked over and thanked Gus for all he had done, she was crying with relief she was free and sorrow for the cost of Luca and Alessandro.

Jake put his arm around Em they turned and walked,

Em stopped and said to Gus. "Oh, I almost forgot, my father, said whatever the operation cost he will fund it."

"That's nice, thank him from me," Gus said, whilst thinking, *payment off Giovanni and Christopher Connaught I will take that.*

"If ever you want a job with those moves of yours Jake, look me up."

"I don't think so, Gus. I will let Em do the ironing." Em looked at Jake quizzically.

"Never mind," Jake said to her.

Gus winked, Jake left with Em.

CHAPTER THIRTY-THREE

December 19th Cheshire 7.00 pm

Jonty glared at Giovanni.
"What is going on Giovanni? How did you sedate me?" Jonty asked.
"We used two tranquilizer guns with darts in them, the same as you see on the TV when they sedate wild animals. We waited in the hedge, at first we could not get a clear shot, once you stood up, we had the perfect opening, and we took it."
"And Bell what about Bell?" Jonty asked.
"He will be Ok when we put you in the van, we rang 999 and asked for an ambulance, we dramatised a little telling them a man was dead in the bushes, it would get them there a little quicker on a cold day."
"You are all heart," Jonty said sarcastically.
"Jonty, this way you get a clear conscience about not working with a crime family" Giovanni paused, "Not taking into account Gus of course."
"How is Emily?" Jonty asked, feeling guilty he had not asked earlier.
"She is fine all went well, Jake and Emily are back together, Billy has fewer men to worry about paying wages to… shall we say! And leave it at that." Giovanni added.
"Talking of Billy, what happened to Jones and Quinn?" Jonty asked.

Giovanni sat back, put a glass of the Bardolino red he chose before taking a sip.

"Jonty you are a policeman and I know it would not look right if my men had assisted you in capturing Billy. How would you explain it?"

"I would have thought of something," Jonty replied

"And with each answer comes another question until eventually, you make a mistake." Giovanni reasoned.

"A genuine friend of the family was murdered, Archbishop Matthew Fitzpatrick, along with an attempt on my life, to make it worse, it was at Roberto's funeral." Giovanni opened.

Jonty never answered he just listened.

"Billy was Roberto's grandson, he was Roberto's shining light, he was the don of the Sartori family."

Giovanni looked sad and down at the table, "I needed to talk to Billy myself about what happened, it was a family affair, not a police issue."

"Giovanni, Billy is a criminal wanted for murder, money laundering, drug trafficking, resisting arrest, gun-running, and many more illegal activities!"

"Maybe in the eyes of the law. Not in the eyes of the family." Giovanni answered.

"Where is Billy now?" Jonty asked hurriedly.

"We entered Billy's house, we did not need force. He trusted me." Giovanni began.

I sat him down in the library, and I asked him if he was responsible for the murder of the Archbishop and the attempted murder of me, as expected he said no, but that doesn't prove he was telling the truth."

"We have an office in the backroom, so we drove Billy here and we did a simple lie detector test on him." Giovanni continued.

"We asked him several questions.

We asked. Were you responsible for the attacks at your grandfather's funeral, Roberto Sartori?
He, answered no! He was telling the truth.

We asked, were you aware of anybody plotting, acting, or generally involved with the attacks at your grandfather Roberto Sartori's funeral?
He answered no! He was telling the truth."
Giovanni took another drink of the Bardolino. "I hope the steak is to your liking Jonty. You have hardly touched it?"
"I'm not hungry! Carry on." Jonty answered bluntly.

"We asked. To your knowledge, did Quinn know of anybody, persons or groups, who were aware of the attack or responsible for the attack at Roberto Sartori's funeral?
He answered no! He was telling the truth.

We asked. Do you know of any reason anybody, person, or group would want to injure, maim or kill Giovanni Sartori and/or Archbishop Matthew Fitzpatrick or anybody linked to them?
He answered no. he was telling the truth."

"What about the kidnap of Emily?" Jonty asked.
"Jonty we considered that. You may see the Sartori family as a crime family, but we have our ethics, laid down by Roberto and I. They were strictly adhered to."

"If Billy had broken any of these rules, he would have paid the penalty for his actions."

"What are those rules, Giovanni?" Jonty asked.

"We grew our business over many years, Jonty – prostitution, and drugs, were no go areas. Most of the families were of the same view. We wanted to protect the working class people not exploit them."

Jonty listened, it was the first time in all his years with the force he had heard any resemblance of ethics from a criminal.

"With this in mind Jonty we asked Billy a few further questions. We could not have our family name attached to drugs in any form."

"We asked Billy during the lie detector test." Giovanni continued

Were you involved in any capacity with the kidnapping of Emily Hughes

He answered no! He was telling the truth.

We asked, are you aware of anybody directly or indirectly involved with the kidnapping of Emily Hughes.

He answered Yes. He was telling the truth."

"Did you say yes then Giovanni, as in Billy knew who was involved in the kidnapping?" Jonty interrupted.

"Yes," Giovanni replied and continued. "After the bank accounts were closed due to the money laundering, Billy could not keep paying his men, and Quinn felt he lost out because his money had stopped and he was stripped of his police pension, following his conduct."

Giovanni took some more Bardolino red on board.

"Quinn and Fitzroy thought of the plan to kidnap Emily and hold her for ransom for three reasons,

They knew Emily's father was rich, so perfect for exploiting.

The kidnap was in America, making it a difficult trail back to them in the UK.

It was a way of getting revenge on Jake and Emily for their involvement in the demise of the business they were running.

Billy turned a blind eye, he could hardly complain, after all the money had ran dry.

Fitzroy took Pitt and O'Neill over to America with him and the rest is history."

"Why did you leave Quinn to be taken by the police and not capture him yourself to question as you did with Billy?" Jonty asked.

"We thought long and hard about that one Jonty. I decided we would probably kill Quinn, but then a part of me thought does that let him off easily? He is a bent cop, He was a superintendent for god's sake," Giovanni continued.

"He will be found guilty of all the charges pressed and he will get a lifetime sentence, I cannot think of a better way to treat Quinn than let all the convicts share a prison cell with a bent cop."

Jonty knew that he meant a crooked police officer's life was horrendous in jail, the convicts took their own laws and used them in their own hands.

"Of course Jonty you cannot charge him for the kidnap that would bring to the forward Gus', mine and your involvement in it."

Jonty nodded in agreement. He knew Giovanni was correct.

"Where is Billy now?" Jonty asked.

"I do not know Jonty, my business with him had concluded. He walked out a free man." Giovanni replied.

"He is a criminal Giovanni, you can't just let him go!" Jonty said forcefully.

"He is a criminal in the eyes of the law, not in the eyes of the family," Giovanni repeated.

"What about the man we saw at the funeral, guiding the helicopter?" Jonty asked.

"We do not know him," Giovanni replied, before continuing. "Find him and it starts our trail onto who is my attempted assassin."

"What happens next?" Jonty asked.

"I am glad you asked Jonty," Giovanni answered.

We have a mutual person to identify and take action against, me for the killing of my friend, the archbishop, and of course, the attempted murder of myself." Giovanni went silent for several seconds.

"You have the same person to find for the same reasons with one difference."

"Which is?" Jonty asked.

"Your reason is to protect the law and bring them to justice."

"And your reason?" Jonty asked.

"Revenge," Giovanni replied, "Revenge!"

"Are you in?"

Jonty replied, I will need one proviso before I agree Giovanni."

"What do you require?" Giovanni asked.

"I also have revenge, revenge that Billy is the murderer of Paul Jennings, the son of my wife." Giovanni listened with his hands clasped over his chest.

"I will want to capture and take Billy in legally, with no interference from you."

"Billy is no longer seen as a member of the family after he arranged the splinter group with Quinn, I have no business with you investigating Billy and prosecuting." Giovanni replied.

He then continued. "So Jonty do we have a deal, are you in or are you out?"

"I'm in," Jonty answered.

***

Christopher Connaught was at home feeling vastly relieved following the last few days of stress and anxiety for the family.

Sat at home with him were Rachael, his wife, Emily and Jake resting in the plush sitting room, the twelve foot high Christmas tree was twinkling with flashing coloured, very tasteful, lights, each had a glass of Italian Bardolino red wine in a Waterford crystal cut glass. He raised his glass and pointed it towards his daughter, Emily, who sat next to Jake on the antique green leather chesterfield opposite the large open fire stocked with a mix of cherry wood, for the fragrance and ash for the heat it gave when burning.

"A toast to the safe return of Emily, I know Jake was involved to some extent, and I do not need to know the detail." He looked at Jake and winked.

"Cheers," Rachael, Emily's Mother, said raising the glass to join in the toast.

As they placed the wine to their lips the telephone rang. "Excuse me a second," Christopher said breaking the restful family reunion for a second.

"Hello Christopher Connaught." He said as he placed the receiver in the customary position from the ear to the mouth.

"Mr Connaught, this is Sheriff John Smith, I have been looking at the file and I believe there are enough grounds to open a case on the disappearance of your daughter Emily."

"Thank you for the call Sheriff, however, I think you were correct last week when you said she will probably turn up, well she has, so there is no need for you to look into the file." Christopher told Sheriff Smith.

"Yes I thought it would be something of nothing," the sheriff said before continuing, "Have a nice Christmas Mr Connaught."

"Merry Christmas Sheriff!"

THE END